THE LAND GRABBERS

They wanted to hang Giles Clanahan for a murder committed by Jake Shockley. To clear his name and bring Shockley to justice, Clanahan flees across the Arizona desert and stumbles across a plot. A band of ex-Confederate soldiers, led by Hammond Cole, plans to seize a valley known as Canoga and drive off the new settlers living there. The only man aware of the plot is Clanahan, and he must play out a bloody game on the open range.

LOGAN WINTERS

THE LAND GRABBERS

Complete and Unabridged

LINFORD
Leicester

First published in Great Britain in 2008 by
Robert Hale Limited
London

First Linford Edition
published 2009
by arrangement with
Robert Hale Limited
London

British Library CIP Data

Winters, Logan.
  The land grabbers. - -(Linford western library)
  1. Western stories.
  2. Large type books.
  I. Title II. Series
  823.9'2–dc22

ISBN 978–1–84782–929–0

Published by
F. A. Thorpe (Publishing)
Anstey, Leicestershire

Set by Words & Graphics Ltd.
Anstey, Leicestershire
Printed and bound in Great Britain by
T. J. International Ltd., Padstow, Cornwall

This book is printed on acid-free paper

1

The three-quarter moon was blue as it drifted overhead across the vast expanse of starry sky. The desert was a silent silver sea, the dunes around me like frozen ocean waves. The going was heavy as I trudged up one side of the sand dunes and waded down again. The night was bitter cold on the Arizona desert, and there was not a sight or sound of life. Earlier, I had heard skulking coyotes raise their plaintive yips to the desolate skies, but they were silent now, curled up in some hidden burrow. I was alone in the night.

There was a dead man behind me, and it seemed that there would be many more of them ahead.

* * *

There was the hum of cicadas down along the river, and something much larger slithered away into the willow brush. There was not a breath of wind blowing, and the desert day, still and hot as it was, was peaceful after the long miles of rough travel I had endured.

The creek flowed evenly, narrow and shallow; my horse and I had water so long as we followed its meandering course. Beyond, the country was yellow and sere, but the river provided some coolness, and here and there stood a shady stand of cottonwoods or live oak trees where we could rest throughout the hottest hours of the day.

This was the Yuma River, flowing eventually past the town of the same name and continuing its snakelike way into Mexico. But I had been told it was also the lifeblood of a small pueblo named Bianca where I expected to meet up again with the killer Jake Shockley.

At noon with the heat of the day beginning to grow intolerable, I did stop in a shady grove beside the river and let my stubby roan pony drink and search the poor forage. Dragonflies sang past and the sand beneath the cottonwoods was alive with insect life. I saw the S-shaped sign of a sidewinder in the sand, but the rattlesnake, too, would have found a cooler place to be with the sun as high as it was. I used my saddle-blanket for a spread and stretched out beneath the trees, hat tilted over my eyes.

About an hour later I was awakened from my doze. Their approach was silent, boots whispering over the sand, but some deep sense alerted me and by the time their shadows fell over me, my hand had already slipped down to the grips of my Colt .44.

I opened my eyes to slits and peered up into the shadows cast by the trees and the brilliance of the sunlight above them. Two men I had never seen before stood looking down at me. Both white, one of them was dressed Mexican-style with a huge sombrero and a tight black vest. The other, a smaller slender man, held a Winchester repeater in his hand, but it was gripped carelessly, not pointed in my direction. Now I slicked the Colt from my holster and sat up.

'Easy, friend,' the bigger man, the one with the wide-brimmed sombrero said, raising his hands a little to show he was not holding a pistol, 'we saw your horse and wondered who you were, that's all.'

'Thought you might be a friend of ours,' the thin man put in, his voice a chirp.

'All right,' I said, rising to my feet. I looked them over and holstered my pistol. They would have taken no offense at my actions. It was a wild time and a wild country. Men didn't stay alive for long by not being alert to their surroundings. 'I'm thinking of boiling up some coffee. You men care to share a pot with me?'

I was hoping to learn more about Bianca from them; they seemed happy to have a cup of coffee. I set to work building a small fire. I suspected that they were opportunists, hoping that my roan had gotten free, that they could catch it up and claim a good day's profit. I had been offered a hundred dollars for the roan the week before in Phoenix, but only laughed at the man although the price was fair enough. There's no way to put a price on a good horse in rough country, and the little roan had done well by me.

Hunkered around the tiny fire, drinking coffee from tin cups, I asked the big man about Bianca. He shook his head, glanced at his friend and said, '*Malo*.' I took it from his response that he and his friend had lived long among the Mexicans, which was accurate. He caught himself and said slowly, his dark eyes glittering under heavy eyebrows, 'That is an outlaw town, my friend. If you have no business there, I would ride wide of it.'

'I have business there,' I answered. I tossed the dregs of my cup on to the fire, watching it hiss and smoke. The two men exchanged another look that I could not penetrate. Maybe they were considering that perhaps I was an outlaw myself, which I was in a way, that perhaps my quick move with my revolver indicated that I was not above murdering them and stealing *their* horses.

At any rate, they did not take long finishing their own coffee, thanking me for it and disappearing into the copse of cottonwoods where they had tied their own ponies.

Hands on hips, frowning, I watched them ride out, their horses' hoofbeats muted by the sand. I had just received my second warning. Bianca was no place for an honest man to enter. John Dancer had told me that before I had even begun my ride south.

'It's a swarming nest of low-lifes and snakes,' was the rancher's estimate of Bianca.

But I had made up my mind. There were things to be accomplished there. One of my deepest failings is that once I have made up my mind, I see things through to the end. It has not always been a trait that has served me well. Time to time people have said that I am 'dogged', but more often they simply call me 'bull-headed'.

No matter, I suppose they come down to the same meaning. I only knew that if I didn't straighten out the whole affair concerning the murder, no law or justice system was ever going to clear my name. My choice had come down to being hanged in Phoenix or shot to pieces in Bianca. At least in Bianca I would have a chance. I saddled my roan once more and continued southward as the sun coasted overhead, beginning its slow descent toward the western mountains.

The roadside sign read 'Campo del Bianca' in barely legible paint. At the foot of the sign a jackrabbit sat panting in the scant shade offered, eyed me briefly and then bounded away. It was still the middle of the afternoon when I reached the low cluster of adobe buildings squatting along the river. No one, nothing was stirring much in the dry heat. I dragged a thin plume of yellow dust behind me down the main street of the tiny pueblo as it dozed on through the hours of siesta.

Few animals were hitched before the business establishments — a weary-looking pair of mules hitched to a rickety wagon in front of the general store, two hard-ridden horses in front of the cantina, a burro looking displaced and irritated at being tied there and neglected. There was nothing unique about the desert town, nothing to encourage hope. Clumps of grease-wood and sage grew along the street, between buildings, wherever they had chosen to take root. Piles of trash cluttered most of the alleyways. A yellow dog got halfway to its feet as if to warn me off, tired of the effort and lay down again in the ribbon of shade it occupied.

Nearer the river I got a hint of Bianca's true aspect. A small rectangular pole corral had been thrown up there beneath the gathered live oak trees and held within it were a dozen of the finest horses you could ever hope to see. Sleek, leggy, deep-chested ponies of all hues. They were expensive mounts, the sort only an outlaw could afford, and needed to outrun more poorly set-up animals local lawmen rode. A quick-looking pinto quarter-horse, a Morgan, a sorrel so well groomed that its hide seemed burnished, a leggy blue roan with a white mane and tail, muscles quivering as it watched me pass, perhaps wanting to run with us, or in challenge to my sturdy, but unremarkable red roan.

Where you might expect a lazy-appearing stableman in a straw sombrero to emerge from the lean-to arrangement that served as the office for the enterprise, here I was met by a red-headed man in a pair of black jeans and pressed white shirt carrying a double-twelve shotgun. He stepped forward to meet me, his eyes searching the area to make sure there were no other men with me. This was no stablehand, but a hired gun paid to stand guard over the valuable animals corralled here.

I smiled, reined in and leaned forward, crossing my hands on the pommel of my battered saddle. The guard did not raise the shotgun toward me, neither did he lower the weapon.

'Can I help you, friend?' he asked, eyeing me narrowly.

'I need to put my pony up,' I answered. 'We've put some miles under us, and he's had nothing but poor fodder for the past few days.'

The man shook his head slightly but definitely from side to side. 'We're full up as you can see.'

'No room for one more tired horse?' I asked in surprise.

'No room. There's a place back uptown called Contrerass. Maybe they can help you.'

There was no threat in his words, but a quiet menace lurked in his eyes and in the way he held his twelve-gauge. This was a private club, it seemed, and no one had issued me an invitation.

I turned my horse away under the steady gaze of the watcher. I was in the right place. That blue roan was Jake Shockley's mount beyond a doubt. He was holed up through the heated hours of day, in a cantina, hotel or some señorita's room, but when the sun dropped lower and the siesta time was past, he would emerge from his hiding place, and I would find him. How I was to handle the six bandits riding with him was something I had not yet determined.

I was thinking that it didn't matter much so long as Jake got his share of frontier justice before they shot me down. Perhaps I just wasn't thinking.

I found the Contrerass Stable and helped the thin twelve-year-old boy there unsaddle and groom my roan. The boy was bright-eyed and eager and he chattered on in rapid Spanish all the time. I caught about one word out of every three as he spun them rapidly off his tongue. But I smiled as if I understood, and gave him a silver dollar as he slipped a nosebag full of oats on to my horse's muzzle. I myself needed a cool place to rest, to eat after the deprivations of the desert trail, but I did not wish to encounter Jake Shockley and his gang just yet — not before I was ready for them.

I wanted to get some food into my belly without showing myself in town so, crouching down I asked the Mexican kid about *comida*, making shoveling movements into my mouth with my fingers. Grinning, he took my hand and led me to a back door, pointing toward a poor adobe house a hundred yards away standing in the shade of twin cottonwood trees.

'*Mi familia*,' he told me, pointing encouragingly toward the house, and I got the idea. Shuffling along the overgrown lane, squinting against the glare of the high sun, I made my way to the door of the house which stood open despite the heat. A trio of gray chickens scratched in the dusty yard and a bearded white goat tied to a stake eyed me dispassionately.

I called to the house several times and eventually a middle-aged lady, round as a ball, wearing a striped many-colored skirt came to the door, wiping her hands on a towel. After a few more gestures and a conversation in broken Spanish and English, the pudgy woman grinned, showing a missing front tooth and escorted me into a low-beamed room which remained cool somehow despite the cooking fire burning in an arched brick fireplace.

'Sit, sit,' my hostess said, and I took off my hat and plumped myself down.

Food was served: tamales, frijoles, tortillas and *chivo* meat, hot and spicy and delicious. I ate voluptuously under her gaze. She beamed at me as if I were doing her a favor. There was a pack of black-eyed kids in the house, and now and then they dared to peek around the corner to watch me enjoying myself at their table.

The lady of the house protested

when I left two silver dollars beside my plate, saying that it was too much, which it might have been, but I was grateful and felt ready to face the world again.

Facing Jake Shockley was another matter.

I stepped out of the shadows of the house into the white sunlight to come face to face with the man I had been chasing. The heavy plank door was slammed shut behind me. The kid from the stable stood just off to my left, still smiling broadly. Now he scooted away through the trees, toward the river.

You'd think that I would have learned somewhere along the road not to trust people for a piece of silver.

Shockley was alone, though I figured there would be more men hidden about. Jake Shockley looked the same as I remembered him: bulky, dirty, wearing a greasy leather vest. His porcine eyes stared at me out of ridges of fat. He had a Winchester repeater in his hands, and I did not believe he held

14

it for decoration.

'Your name's Clanahan, isn't it?' he said slowly, 'Giles Clanahan — isn't that right?'

I nodded carefully. There was no denying it, though I wished I could have. Shockley's thick finger was fitted into the trigger guard of the Winchester, curled around the curved trigger. I noticed that the rifle's hammer was drawn back. Had I the quickest draw in Arizona Territory, he still would have shot me down before I could clear leather, and at that range the rifle bullet could cut my spine in half.

Shockley's amused little eyes continued to survey me. He spat without turning his head and a gob of tobacco juice landed near my boot. 'Well, well,' Shockley said.

'I've been wanting to have a look at the man who killed me. Frankly, you don't look up to it.'

He whistled shrilly then, and from behind the house two riders emerged to side Shockley. Both were angry-looking, red-eyed, probably having been roused from their siestas. One of the two led the blue roan with the white mane and tail, and Shockley accepted the reins to the leggy animal.

'Take that side arm off him, Curt,' Shockley ordered. 'I wouldn't want Mr. Clanahan to kill me again.' He emitted a muffled snort, something close to a laugh, but not exactly that. Jake Shockley, it seemed, was not much experienced in laughing.

The tall, shabby-looking man named Curt slid easily from his saddle, half-turned me and lifted my Colt from its holster. I say that Curt was shabby in appearance, but beyond his personal appearance everything gleamed with hints of wealth. The black Morgan horse I had seen at the riverside corral was decked out in a silver-mounted saddle and bridle. His gunbelt where two .36 Remingtons rode was decorated with silver conches. The pistols themselves had ivory grips.

The second rider approached me on

his paint pony, formed a noose in his lariat, draped it over my shoulders and backed his horse to tighten it so that the rope cut into my arms and chest.

'Let's take Mr. Clanahan for a little walk, boys,' Jake Shockley said, and I was jerked away from the house in a staggering, stumbling run. I had to keep my feet or the trotting horse would have dragged me, face-first over the rocky earth. I had never realized before just how difficult it is to run without the use of your arms. I thought of that and then released the thought, using all of my concentration simply trying to stay upright. Jake Shockley glanced back at me and smiled with satisfaction.

I had done everything wrong. Riding into the outlaw town, I had first gone to the bandits' stable and announced my presence in Bianca. Then I had let the guard posted there send me to another stable I knew nothing about. Had let the kid send me to a house for my last meal, giving Jake Shockley time to be alerted, to gather his crew, to capture me.

The rope, binding me like iron bands, gave me pause to consider what it might feel like around my neck.

We had come once again to the sandy river banks. The river flowed past flat, shallow and smooth, mirroring the high sun. The cicadas fell mute as we followed the riverside trail The horses had been slowed to a walk so that I was able to follow along without fear of falling. I kept quiet. What was the use of protesting, cursing or begging?

'What are you taking all this trouble for, Jake?' the outlaw riding the paint pony asked in a querulous voice. 'It's hot out. Shoot him and give some Mex two dollars to plant him. Besides we should be heading out for Canoga.'

'There's justice in it this way,' Jake Shockley answered heavily. 'This man, this Clanahan, is the one who killed me over to Mesa Grande. Oh, that's right, you weren't there, were you, Vallejo? Curt was — tell him, Curt.'

'You're doing fine,' the equally-irritated Curt replied. Both of Shockley's minions obviously felt that their time could be better spent elsewhere. Jake Shockley continued:

'Me and Curt, a few of the boys were dining on red beans and whiskey when a stranger walked into the saloon in Mesa Grande. Curt says, 'Jake, don't that gent look like you?' Well, I didn't think so. A man never thinks another looks like him. But the more I watched the fellow, I began to see a resemblance. Heavy, with a bearded face. I began to think of the possibilities.'

Jake's voice was flat, the way he told the story was uninteresting to the other outlaws. But not to me. We halted in the shade of some shaggy willow trees. Jake removed his hat, wiped at his brow with a bandana and returned to his story-telling.

'Curt had got me to thinking,' he said, 'thinking about the posters that were out on me, about the warrants running all the way back to El Paso. I waited until the stranger was half-drunk. When he left the saloon, we followed him.

'We steered him into an alley and I laid him out with the muzzle of my Colt. Then I lifted his pistol. I meant to leave my own revolver behind — you know that old six-shooter of mine, the one with my initials carved into the handle? That and an old folded-up wanted poster on me that I shoved into his vest pocket. Then we waited.'

'After a while here comes our friend Mr. Clanahan up the alley, leading his horse. I stepped out and yelled something — don't recall what — and fired my gun into the stranger's heart.'

'Clanahan fired back, but he had no clear shot and was taken unaware. He might have hit the sky, nothing else.' Jake took a drink from his canteen and passed it around to the others.

'People came running, naturally. Me and Curt just sauntered away.'

'All right,' Vallejo grumbled. The water was not doing the job for him. He obviously had other places he'd rather be, other drinks he would prefer, other things he'd rather be doing than sitting in the heat listening to Jake's rambling story. 'You shot a man? So?'

'I didn't shoot a man, Vallejo. Clanahan did. And the man he shot was Jake Shockley, don't you see? What happened next was funny. They were all glad-handing Clanahan here for killing a wanted outlaw. They gave him a reward for the shooting. Isn't that right, Clanahan.'

I didn't answer. What was the point in it? The dry wind whipped the perspiration from my back and chest before it could form. My mouth was as dry as the desert sand. I eyed the slowly running river, blue along the banks, silver-bright, dancing with highlights the sun painted on its surface in the middle. Jake was taking his time, enjoying himself.

'Two days later they were ready to hang Mr. Clanahan. Some folks came into town looking for a missing man.

They identified the body and things got angry while they tried to decide if Clanahan had maybe made a mistake, or known all along that he wasn't Jake Shockley, and been looking for a way to make some easy money. Either way they had it in mind to hang him for the murder . . . how'd you escape, Clanahan?'

I still said nothing. I didn't care to add to the entertainment at what was to be my own funeral.

'If I'd escaped,' Jake said, halting his horse again near a sycamore tree with heavy, low-hanging boughs, 'I would have made for the border. Why chase after me, Clanahan?' He shook his head heavily and said, 'You are a man of little sense.'

Then, abruptly, he stopped. 'That one will do, Curt,' he said, pointing up at a mottled branch ten feet overhead. 'Flip that rope over.'

It was then or never. Curt swung down, and doing so he loosened the rope just a bit. I hit the ground, shrugging out of the noose. I felt it slide up and over my ears, heard Jake yell, heard the report of his Winchester, but by then I had legged it the few yards to the river and plunged into it, swimming for all I was worth. Bullets fanned the water around me and I dove, swimming toward the far shore with all of my strength, lungs bursting. The river was carrying me away, the current much swifter than I had guessed. I had to come up for air; my lungs felt ready to explode, and when I rose gasping, I saw that I was a hundred yards downstream from the lynch mob.

One of them spotted me and cried out and I saw them race for leather, flagging their horses after me. Taking three deep breaths, I went under again and let the current take me, propelling me along much faster than I could have swum.

Coming up for air again, I saw that the beach where the outlaws rode was being pinched by a rising red bluff, leaving them no riverside trail to follow. They had drawn up in an angry knot.

Bullets flew, wild and high, echoing distantly. I dove under once more.

When I came to the surface again, I saw no one across the river. The red bluff dominated the skyline, casting a heavy shadow across the river. On my side of the river the land was flat, white sand and low, dry willow brush. I tried to stand, was knocked from my feet by the current and tried again. Finally I was able to wade to the beach and stagger away from the river.

My lungs were burning, I didn't have enough strength to run and so I staggered and stumbled on like a drunken man across the heated sand, looking back all the while. They might have crossed the river on horseback, they might appear around the last bend at any moment.

But I didn't think that Jake Shockley would just give it up. Not from what I knew of the man.

He would track me down if he could, ride me into the ground and then he would try to hang me again.

24

2

I had seen the long miles of dunes when I crested out the low knolls along the river. Desolate and forbidding, there was no water, no vegetation to be seen. Only an endless sea of white sand stretching in every direction for as far as the eye could see. No man could cross them afoot, not without water. But neither could any horse. Its weight would drag it into the dunes up to its belly, leaving it thrashing and panicked, useless to any rider. The choice then being between returning to the river where I would certainly be run down eventually and striking out across the blistering dunes was no choice at all.

They might one day find my bleached bones on the desert, but they would not find them with a noose around its neck. I went on through the dazzling light of day, the sand scorching my feet through my boots which, ironically, were still soaked with river water.

I walked on, with no goal but escape. Dizzy and dehydrated, my legs growing heavier with each mile, each attempt to scale one more ridge of dunes, I continued, praying for darkness. Night would be cold, chillingly cold, but anything would be a welcome relief from the mocking glare of the sun.

Two dark specks and then a third, a fourth, appeared overhead and I was spurred onward. I would not give my flesh up to the gathering vultures. Night came and passed — or so I imagined until I realized that I had passed out and fallen face-first into the sand. Night was still hours away — if I could make it that long, I thought that somehow I could survive. The gathering vultures had become a swarm, a dark cloud patiently hanging overhead.

I walked on. The sky began to dim. There was a hint of palest crimson along the western horizon and deep violet shadows began to creep into the contours of the dunes. My tongue was glued to my palate; my legs were rubbery and leaden at once. My vision cleared only when I squinted my eyes as hard as possible. I saw the evening star blink on, glowing dully through the haze of color the sunset washed across the sky.

I walked on, following the star to the west.

After midnight there were a million stars, so silvery-thick that you could hardly see black sky between them. I could pick out the Dipper easily enough, and keeping it on my right shoulder, I continued westward. Hours passed, days, years, and I continued on, wading through the calf-high sand. Sometime halfway between midnight and dawn the land began to level. I could feel rough stones underfoot now, and I entered yet another dream world. Saguaro cactuses, twenty-feet high or more, stood with their arms elevated like felons caught in a raid.

I tripped, stumbled, fell on my face and scraped it against the volcanic rock beneath me. I rose only with extreme effort, my mind shouting at my body that we must continue on or die here. My body paid little attention, but still I managed to draw myself to my feet somehow and walked on, moving in a weaving line.

I thought I could make out the dark bulk of low hills ahead of me, but they were far distant. Depleted, beaten down I focused my eyes on one star low on the horizon and started heavily onward. The star flickered before my eyes, seemed to change color, to flare up and brighten. I was watching the end of days, no longer so much walking as dragging my boots on the ends of my legs.

The star grew brighter, again changed color and I closed my eyes, tightly, trying to squeeze them to cogency. But when I opened them, the star continued to flare and flicker and change colors. Crimson and gold, then orange and twisting tendrils of black.

It was a campfire that I had been watching. My heart gave a leap. I would have run if I could have. I didn't care whose fire it was, what manner of men were gathered there. At that moment I didn't even care if it proved to be Shockley — let them hang me, it made no difference any more. Dying couldn't be any worse than what I had endured on the desert this day.

Staggering, appearing like an apparition out of the night, I entered the camp and fell to my face. Someone grabbed me by the shoulders, rolled me over and splashed water on my sun-ravaged face. It was like a gift from the gods. I tried to stifle the groan which rose from my throat, but it escaped my blistered lips.

'Get up, mister!' a deep voice commanded. My moment of grace ended as quickly as it had begun.

'Don't know . . . if I can,' I said.

'Can't you see the shape he's in?' another voice asked, a softer voice. 'He can't be scouting for them.'

'Why not?' the deeper voice demanded. 'Just because he's in bad shape?'

'Little water,' I managed to say and again the canteen was lowered, this time applying a few drops to my mouth. My swollen tongue sucked at it greedily.

'Ask him who he is!' yet another voice said.

'Find out if he knows where they are.'

I had no idea what they were talking about, these voices, these shadows in the night. Someone helped me to sit up and I opened my eyes, squinting into what now seemed the fierce glow of a campfire. There were covered wagons around me and five or six men in Army uniforms watching me warily, rifles in their hands.

The officer in charge raked me with his dark eyes and asked, 'What happened to you?'

I lied because the true story would have taken too long, was impossible to believe and might even have gotten me taken back to Mesa Grande to be hung.

'Apaches.'

'We haven't heard of any in the area. What band were they? White Mountain? Chiricahua?'

'I don't know how to tell the difference,' I said honestly. 'I'm not a soldier. More water, please. Just a drop or two.'

'Let him have some water, for God's sake,' the softer voice that I had heard earlier said, and I shifted my eyes to see that it was indeed a woman standing there, her face hidden in the confused shadows of starlight and fire-smoke, but sounding young, appearing slender. Her arms were folded beneath her breasts.

'Captain?' one of the soldiers inquired before tipping the canteen again.

'We have little enough,' the officer said stiffly, 'but I wouldn't let a dog die of thirst out here.'

With that he turned his back to me, took the young woman by the elbow and marched off across the camp clearing. I could now make out the man with the canteen. He was thick through the chest and the feeble firelight revealed the three gold sergeant's stripes on his blue uniform. He held my head and gave me a few more sips of water.

'You'd better take it easy with that for awhile,' he said not unkindly.

'Sergeant?' I asked. 'What did the captain mean when he asked if I was 'one of them'? Who are *they*?'

The big man hesitated then replied, 'If you are one of them you already know, if you aren't you don't need to know. Refer your questions to Captain Cole.'

It was hardly a satisfying answer, but at the moment it seemed unimportant, so I let it go.

'I'll find you a blanket and a place to stretch out,' the sergeant said, rising to his feet. 'Morning's time enough to ask questions.'

Someone shoved a blue army blanket into my hands, I was hoisted to my feet and deposited beneath the tailgate of a wagon. I thought it was one of the most wonderful places I had ever been. A blanket, an army guard, water. I ached too much to sleep, to think of sleep. I needed it too much for it to be denied and in minutes I was wrapped in a dark, comforting cocoon, uncaring and, for the moment, quite content just to be alive.

Morning, when it came with a lurid splash of color across the eastern skies, the sounds of men and horses stirring, was a different story.

My eyes were glued shut with sleep, and I was first aware of the throbbing pain in my feet. My water-soaked boots had shrunken with the blazing heat of the desert sands and they were holding my swollen feet in an iron grip. I could cut them off, I thought, and walk in what? As I managed to rub the sleep from my raw eyes, I became aware of two things simultaneously — a head-ache of magnificent proportions rushed through my skull, threatening to explode it, and a soldier, dark and vague in silhouette against the harsh colors of dawn sat on an upturned crate nearby, a

Springfield rifle across his knees, watching me.

'Got any water?' I managed to ask through my parched, split lips. That was still my primary concern. I wondered how much weight a body, unreplenished by water, would lose after ten hours of hundred-degree heat. I actually tried to calculate that, failed and gave it up as the soldier handed me his canteen. I uncorked it, rinsed my mouth and drank two hard swallows. I remembered someone saying that they were short on water and so I recorked the canteen and handed it back to the man, though I am sure I could have easily drunk its entire contents.

The soldier, a corporal, I saw as my vision organized itself, looked more relieved than annoyed with me. He must have been sitting there for many hours through the cold desert night. He stood, shouldered his canteen and yelled across his shoulder:

'Sergeant Hawkins! Billy — find

Hawkins and tell him that the prisoner is awake.'

Prisoner? Was I now a prisoner of the army? For what reason? I convinced myself that the guard had only used that term because he had obviously been posted to watch me and it was the term he associated with that duty.

The corporal stood glowering over me, but I thought that it was only the duty he hadn't liked, not me personally. Sergeant Hawkins, who I recognized by shape and by the chevrons on his sleeves from the night before, approached after another few minutes. He was graying, and I suspected, balding beneath his army cap. His face was the odd mixture of command and compassion that I supposed was necessary in a good non-commissioned officer.

'All right, Gentry,' he said to the corporal, 'Get yourself some coffee before it's all gone. I'll take charge of the prisoner.'

There was that word again. How could I be a prisoner? What was I convicted of? Accused of. Again I convinced myself that it was only terminology, there being no word to define a desert wretch who had invaded their night camp. I was, at the very least, suspicious. I knew that I hadn't sold my story about being attacked by Apaches well the previous night. They still seemed convinced that I was one of *them*. It was useless to try explaining that I had no idea who *they* were.

'Can you get up?' the big sergeant asked, bending over me.

'I guess I'll have to,' I said, manufacturing a weak grin, 'if I don't want to get left behind.' Groaning with the effort I sat, turned and gripped the edge of the tailgate, pulling myself erect. Turning, I faced Hawkins. The huge red sun was stunning to my eyes as it floated up over the dunes. My legs were not wobbly — it was as if they were not even there. My feet I was well aware of, swollen and blistered, encased in shrunken leather, they gave the sensation of standing in a caldron of molten metal. Hawkins frowned.

'You've got to get those boots off,' he said.

'And run around barefoot?'

'I'll find you a pair of boots,' the NCO offered. 'For now, let's feed you something.' He inclined his head toward the campfire where four or five soldiers were standing, eating pan bread, drinking coffee.

'I don't think I could hold it down,' I said honestly. 'Coffee, if you've enough.'

'All right, come along then.'

I didn't want to let go of the tailgate, but I forced myself to and I followed after the sergeant in a hobbling gate. Now I was aware of my leg muscles again — knotted and strained. I went stiffly on, feet burning. I touched my forehead and found a wide scrape there. It was a minute before I remembered having fallen.

The soldiers around the campfire eyed me suspiciously. Sergeant Hawkins poured and handed me a cup of hot coffee which I drank with shaking hands. All around other troopers were hitching the horse teams, saddling their own mounts. I didn't dawdle over the coffee, seeing that they were anxious to be moving. Hawkins told me to wait near the wagon where I had slept and I staggered that way.

Hawkins caught up with me minutes later, astride a bay army horse. There was something in his hand and he tossed me a pair of scuffed cavalry boots.

'I took you for a size eight, so I brought you tens,' he said. 'You might not want to put them on for awhile even so. Get up on the tailgate and perch there. We'll be pulling out in ten minutes.'

'Whose . . . ?' I asked, looking at the boots.

'Don't worry about it. He won't be needing them any more.'

With the ball of the red sun in my eyes I pulled myself up on to the tailgate of what I now saw was a supply

38

wagon filled with barrels of flour and sacks of oats, miscellaneous hardware. With my skinning knife I got to work on my boots. The sharp, curved blade, meant for skinning deer and other game, sawed with little trouble from the top of my boots to the arch. Peeled open like that I was able to spread the baked leather and remove them, sliding the boots carefully over the blisters there. It was painful enough, but the relief of bringing my feet out into fresh air made it worth it.

I removed my foot rags and scowled down at the shape my feet were in. Shriveled yet swollen. There was a blister the size of a silver dollar on each heel and across my toes was a row of white blisters like pale knuckles.

Someone yelled; the man driving the freight wagon cracked his whip and the wagon lurched forward, moving north-ward over the rough earth which was strewn with black volcanic rock. Now I began to grow hungry and wished I had eaten something at the cookfire. My feet, swollen and aching, continued to burn. I was sore all over and weak as a pup, as if my skeleton had dissolved on me.

I watched the cavalrymen behind and to the side of me. They were grim to a man. I saw by their unshaven faces and the dust on their uniforms that they had been on the trail for a long time. Their horses were weary as they plodded on across the barren landscape where only cholla cactus, stunted sage and an occasional shaggy Joshua tree grew.

The girl appeared out of nowhere, riding an off-white gelding. Slowing, she came even with the tailgate and with the agility of a circus rider, swung from the saddle and on to the tailgate to sit beside me.

'Too darn hot,' she said, tilting back her broad-brimmed black hat to dab at her forehead with a lace-edged handkerchief. She was smaller than I had thought, dark-eyed, dark hair tied up in one long braid that hung down her back nearly reaching her waist. She looped her horse's reins around one of the chains that supported the tailgate and smiled at me.

'I'm Beth Cole,' she said, offering a gloved hand which I took. Her black eyes watched me questioningly. Her voice was pleasant, faintly Southern.

'Gi . . . Jim Clampett,' I stuttered. Her eyes narrowed in amusement. Perhaps she was used to men losing their tongues when talking to her. I suppose Beth was no artist's model, no angelic creature — her nose was a little too short, her mouth too generous for perfectionist — but she was a striking woman, and her eyes, dancing with inner merriment were enough to make you swallow hard before you spoke. Even if you weren't lying, which I was because I had no idea if the law was still looking for me for the murder of one Joseph Carter in Mesa Grande. I assumed they were. These small towns don't take kindly to strangers riding in and gunning down respectable citizens.

41

Unfortunately, I had completely botched my only chance at clearing myself by taking Jake Shockley back to stand trial for the murder.

'How far did you walk!' Beth said, noticing my feet as I held one of them up for inspection.

'I don't know. A day and a night.'

'After the Apaches jumped you.'

'That's right,' I answered.

'Do you want to talk about it?' she asked, leaning closer to me.

'No. It wasn't pretty,' I said. I didn't want to try to invent a long, complicated lie and get caught up in it. 'Are you the captain's . . . ?'

'Sister? Yes I am,' Beth answered. 'If you're asking if he will like it when he sees me sitting here with you, the answer is no, he will not.' The wagon jounced over a large rock and she instinctively grabbed my arm. Only for a moment.

'Could you tell me?' I asked carefully, 'Who *they* are? The people the soldiers are so wary of.' By the way the troopers rode, not in file, but spread out across the raw land, it was obvious that they were expecting trouble from some quarter and were doing their best to be ready for it.

'You don't know?' she asked in surprise.

'No. No one would tell me.'

She tilted her head back and a melodic little laugh rose from her throat. 'Boy, are you in the wrong place! You thought you had Apache trouble — wait until you see what comes next. They'll probably hang you along with the rest of them.'

I shook my head, trying to clear it. I still didn't understand, and it seemed that it was in my best interests to know.

'Who will hang us? Who, Beth? You have to tell me who they are, please.'

'Why the army of course,' she said. 'You don't think they're going to let us get away with this!'

3

I studied the woman carefully. The morning sunlight was brilliant behind her, leaving her face in shadow. I could see the gleam in her eyes, however, and the flash of white teeth as her expression brightened, faded and then brightened again, less convincingly.

'I'm starting to believe that you don't know anything about what's going on,' Beth said.

'You should believe that, since I don't. I would appreciate it if someone told me something.'

'What have the others told you?' Beth asked.

'No one's told me anything! Except for Sergeant Hawkins. He said that if I was one of them I already knew, if I wasn't, I didn't need to know.'

'I guess,' Beth said thoughtfully, 'that he was right. I'm sure he was,' she added more definitely. After another quarter of a mile of bouncing along on the wagon's tailgate she turned those dark eyes on me again and asked:

'If you're not one of those army scouts, what were you doing out here?'

'Doing?' The truth might get me hanged. On the other hand, nobody believed my story of having been attacked by a party of Apaches. I shrugged indifferently, 'There are such things as coincidences, Beth.'

'Of course,' she said. 'But out here!' Her hand gestured toward the limitless desert. 'It seems unlikely.' She confided, 'It would be better for you to come clean when they ask you again. Otherwise you will remain a prisoner. Worse,' she said soberly, 'they might decide to set you free. Without a horse, without water, with your feet in the shape they are.' I saw an approaching rider, an angry Captain Cole on his leggy palomino mare.

'If I were you,' Beth said in a near-whisper, 'I'd come up with a lie

45

that has a chance of sticking.'

'Get off of there, Beth,' Cole's voice boomed. His pretty little palomino tossed its head as he slowed it to match the wagon's pace. 'What's the idea? Fraternizing with the prisoner!' His lean face was so red that it nearly matched his russet mustache. His pale eyes were narrowed with anger.

'Calm yourself, Hammond,' Beth said lightly. 'It's already hot. At least there's some shade from the canvas here, and sitting that horse is starting to rub me raw.'

Captain Hammond Cole settled his glare on me as if he wanted to accuse me of something, but couldn't quite figure out what. In the end he just muttered at me, 'Be careful. You're on the ragged edge.' Then to his sister, 'Come on. I want you to ride point with me.'

Beth stretched her arms, nodded, untied the reins to her pony, and then as agilely as she had dismounted, swung back on to the white horse's back, smiled faintly at me and rode away, following her brother.

If that was who he was.

At least among people like Jake Shockley, a man knew where he stood. Among these soldiers who might or might not have been soldiers who had other soldiers chasing them, or said they did, with a determination to deny me any information, how was I to know who to believe, to trust — if anyone?

I began to plan how to steal a horse and slip away.

That was a hanging offense under frontier law since leaving a man afoot in hostile territory was the same as murdering him. If caught I would have yet another group wanting to stretch my neck. I had the law in Mesa Grande, the outlaw Jake Shockley and soon, if I was not lucky, the army. It was only soldiers, I thought, who were taken before an execution squad. Common thieves were hanged.

Which gave me a moment's thought. Beth had said that if they were caught they would all likely hang. Did that bolster my notion that these were not soldiers at all, but men who had somehow come by the cavalry trappings? I did not know, and I no longer cared. I no longer cared about the soldiers, if that was what they were, about *them*, whoever *they* might be. It was obvious that I was in a situation where I did not belong and that it could only get worse. What had Beth said?

'If you thought you had trouble with the Apaches, wait until you see what comes next.'

I did not wish to stay around and find out what she meant. I was determined to risk all and escape if possible.

I brooded, dozed, tended my feet throughout the morning. From time to time, troopers would approach the supply wagon to dip their canteens into the water barrels which were carried one on either side. I listened to snatches of conversation, partly to relieve the boredom, partly in hopes of gathering information. Most of what I overheard was simply grumbling about the heat, the food, the long ride. Once, though, I did hear Corporal Gentry tell another soldier that he estimated that they would reach Canoga early the next afternoon.

'None too soon for me,' the trooper replied.

'It'll be worth it in the end, Kent. Wait until you see how much . . . '

Their voices faded as, with their canteens refilled, they swung their horses away from the wagon.

Canoga. Why did that ring a dull bell in the back of my mind? I had never been to such a place, nor heard of it before. Was it a town, a general term for the area? I squinted my eyes, trying to remember because it seemed that it might be important. It came to me in a flash, hardly enlightening, but bringing a chill with it:

Canoga. One of the outlaws riding with Jake Shockley after he had decided that it would give him pleasure to lynch me had said, 'What are you taking all this trouble for, Jake . . . we should be heading for Canoga.' I was sure of it. The one called Vallejo, the one who rode a paint horse. I could almost see his face as he protested the morning's entertainment.

Did Shockley and his rough band of men have a rendezvous with this bedraggled army? Or was he and his gang the *them* the army feared? No matter, I was more determined than ever to make my escape before they decided just who was to have the honor of hanging me.

They made camp at the hour of sundown. Horses and men had been driven to their limit through the smoldering hours of the desert day. Ragged-looking now, dead tired, the soldiers straggled in toward the camp-fires, wanting the reviving food and sleep.

I was on my feet, sore as they were, wandering the camp perimeter. No one kept watch over me any more. If I got away, so much the better. The desert would deal with me sooner or later. Someone — Captain Cole, I assumed — had determined that I wasn't worth tying up or hanging. Besides, there wasn't a tree for twenty miles in any direction.

All day I had been plotting my escape. Finally, I settled on a plan that seemed reckless, but had the quality of simplicity. If it worked, fine. If it did not, I had lost nothing. It was a desperate plan, yes, but then I was a desperate man. Near the remuda where the weary horses had been picketed, I waited. As the sun lowered in the west, becoming a flattened red ball which spewed out purple and deep-blue coloring across the long desert as it died, I watched as a straggler made his way toward the camp. The trooper was a narrow man with a dark mustache and red-rimmed eyes. I walked out to meet him.

'What's your name?' I asked as he drew up his bay. His hard eyes narrowed.

51

'Kirk,' he replied. 'What makes it your business?'

'The captain sent me over to wait for you.' I inclined my head toward Cole's wagon. 'He wants to see you.'

'What about?' he asked suspiciously.

'I wouldn't know, friend. We're hardly on intimate terms. He just said to find Kirk and have him report to the wagon.'

Kirk, bone-weary, wishing for nothing more than coffee and beans himself, growled and swung down while I held his horse's bridle. He breathed out a few harsh curses, dusted himself off and said, 'Take care of my horse.'

I nodded as he started toward Cole's wagon, his steps stiff with the long day's riding.

Then I swung into the saddle of the bay horse, heeled it sharply into a gallop and rode from the camp, bent low across the withers. I heard a shout and someone unleashed a shot in my general direction, but the bullet came nowhere near me. I rode the tired horse on unmercifully at a run for nearly a mile, then slowed, halted, and looked back toward the camp from the back of the shuddering bay.

There was no pursuit. I expected none. The exhausted soldiers would not be eager to saddle up again and ride after me in the settling darkness where pursuit would likely prove futile anyway. Nor, I thought, would Cole care enough to order them to follow. The only man who would be angry enough at me to attempt it was Kirk who probably would receive a dressing-down for his carelessness, but he no longer even had a mount and it seemed unlikely he could sustain his anger for long.

I started on, walking the weary horse through the falling twilight. I did not know where I was riding. I knew I would not try the dunes again, not try to double back and tempt fate. Ahead. I rode northward, pointing the stumbling pony's nose toward Polaris.

There were still a few ounces of water in Kirk's canteen, and I swallowed half of it as I rode. Water, I knew, was my next need. Freedom on the desert was an illusion without water. I had a thousand square miles of uncharted wasteland surrounding me. I did not know the land: I doubted if more than a few dozen white men did.

We trudged on through the night, the poorly-used bay horse and I, as the temperature beneath a brutally clear sky began to fall.

It was close to midnight, at a guess, when I rode the struggling bay up a low knoll dotted with agave and buffalo grass when I felt the horse quiver and stall beneath me. I feared at first that it was close to foundering, but that was not the case.

It perked its ears and blew explosively through its nostrils, tugging at the reins, wishing to travel westward. I let the horse have its head.

The silver half-moon only now had begun to slip toward the skies from behind the western mountains, and travel became easier by its glow. The mysterious shadows I had jumped at earlier now became landforms, rocks, an occasional saguaro or mesquite tree. And by the light of the moon I saw what had beckoned the horse.

A pond appearing no larger than a dinner plate gleamed in the moonlight. Crowding its shore were cattails and willow brush. Three larger trees, twisted, and solemn, stood nearby. We hit the flats and moved toward the water, the bay fighting me all the way in his eagerness to drink.

Another fifteen minutes brought us to the pond. We startled a few night-birds in our passing. The trees — sycamores I now saw — loomed dark and barren above us, casting intricate shadows across the raw earth.

'Let that animal drink the water and he's dead,' a voice from behind the trees said. 'And if you don't ride out now, there's a chance you'll die too.'

I reined in the bay and waited. The shadowy figure moved toward me. A Sharps carbine accompanied it. The finger caressing the trigger of the .56 was too nervous for my liking. It also belonged to a small hand connected to the slender arm of a girl with a tangle of fuzzy hair. Illuminated by the silver of the moon, it formed a wild aureole around her shadowed face.

'I said, ride!' the girl said. I shook my head.

'The horse can't take anymore. I'm not sure I can.'

There was a moment of considered silence and then she said, 'Well, swing down then. If you've got any guns, shuck 'em.'

'I'm unarmed,' I said, knowing that would sound odd. What sane man would ride this wild country without a weapon? He would have to be a fool or a man in serious trouble. I supposed I was some of each.

Carefully, I dismounted, keeping a tight grip on the reins; the bay continued to strive toward water.

'It's arsenic poisoned,' the girl said, waving a hand toward the pond. 'There was a warning sign, but we didn't see it in the dark. Nor the dead bones scattered about.'

She came nearer. No more than five feet tall, she seemed overmatched by the Spencer repeater, but she appeared more than familiar with the weapon. Her eyes narrowed still more as she examined the bay, running her hand over it from neck to quivering flank.

'I hate you!' she screamed at me, and the muzzle of the rifle fixed itself on me. I could see her breast rising and falling, see the anger in her eyes by the mirrored light of the silver moon.

'Hold on,' I said, involuntarily raising my hands. 'I don't know you, lady. You don't know me. You have no reason to hate me.'

'I know who you are,' she said with bitter, choppy words. 'One of *them*.'

I was tired of being one of them. Everyone believed that I was . . . whatever I was supposed to be. '*Who*,' I asked, 'do you think I am?'

'This tells me,' she said, and I saw

her finger trace the US brand on the bay horse's hip. 'Don't tell me that you're a soldier!' she said, laughing explosively. There was no humor behind the expression.

'I stole the horse,' I said, resorting to the truth. 'I needed it to escape from some men back there. I don't know who they are either, but they are not regular army. That much was made obvious to me.'

She seemed to relax just a little, I took a chance and lowered my hands. 'So you're not an outlaw, but just a horse thief,' she said. Again she laughed, a little nervously, I thought.

'That's right. Look . . . whatever your name is . . . it's a long story, but whoever, whatever you think I am, I am not. Maybe we could talk it over. If you don't mind my commenting on it — this is a hell of a place to find a woman alone.'

'I was not alone when I started,' she said. She was trying to keep her voice firm, but there was a slight quavering there. The rifle in her hands, however, seemed as resolute as ever. She sighed and shook her head. 'You'd better tie the bay. The water is poison, and he's the only horse we have now.'

I tethered the unhappy bay to a low-hanging branch of one of the sycamore trees, loosened the cinches and took Kirk's canteen from the saddlehorn. All under the muzzle of the tiny girl's large-bore rifle.

Beyond the trees, the girl still holding the rifle at my back, I found her poor camp. And not twenty feet from it was a sandy hummock with a cross made from twigs. Around the pond, I now saw by moonlight the bleached bones of a dozen animals — deer, coyote, a puma and at least one steer. In the pale glow of the moon it had an eerie effect on me. Reminders of mortality can have that effect.

'Sit down,' the girl instructed, and I nodded. Seeing a blanket spread across the ground I lowered myself. My feet in the oversized cavalry boots still throbbed and burned, but that seemed inconsequential now. The girl — woman, if barely that — sat nearby on a broken tree stump. I noticed that she was eyeing the canteen I had brought. Casually, I flipped it toward her.

'There's not much in it,' I apologized.

'More than I've had in — ' She tilted the canteen to her lips and drank deeply. Ashamedly she started to push the cork back in.

'Go ahead,' I said. 'Take another.'

With murmured gratitude, she did so. I watched her speculatively. What I had said earlier was true enough — this was no place for a woman wandering alone. Even if she had begun with a companion, why had they come out into this desolate land?

She sat on the tree stump, her legs sheathed in black jeans, crossed at the ankles, the Spencer across her knees. Her face, I could see now with the moonlight fully on it, was still in that changing stage between rounded girl-ishness and the more well-defined lines

60

of womanhood. She could have been anywhere from sixteen to eighteen years old, no more I thought. The wild halo of hair lighted now by moon shine seemed more blond than I had thought. Her mouth was small, almost delicate, her eyes wide. I could not determine their color, but they were expressive and sad, all of her earlier anger drained from them.

'What happened?' I asked after a long minute of silence. Without gesturing, I indicated the hummock.

'My father,' she said with a sniff, a catch in her throat. 'Our horses were so terribly thirsty . . . we were so terribly thirsty. Father drank deeply from the water, remarking on its bitter taste which he took for the alkali that is so common in the area in standing water. I had busied myself first unsaddling the horses and stacking our belongings to one side.'

'The sun was high and hot. I led the horses to water and let them drink. Looking around, I realized that Father had said nothing for a long time. When I found him, he was holding his stomach, writhing on the ground. I tried to comfort him. He muttered something about the horses and I realized that it was the water. That Father was sick from it and I was letting the horses fill their bellies with the same stuff. I drew them away from it, but it was too late. In minutes they had fallen, legs thrashing, foaming at the mouth.'

'Only then did I see the crooked sign someone had posted. It had fallen over, its post rotted away. 'Poison Water', it warned. By then Father was dying, his skin dry as parchment, his tongue — '

She broke down then, buried her face in her hands and sobbed, the emotion racking her thin shoulders. The rifle dropped to the ground, ignored. I understood now what had happened. But not *why* it had. What sort of man would bring his young daughter out on to the faceless desert, putting her life and his own at risk? The scent of desperation lingered here. I needed to know:

'What is it that is happening here? What is going on in Canoga? Who are these people in army uniforms?' I asked quietly after she had recovered herself. 'What has it all to do with you . . . and *who* are you?'

4

'My name is Patricia Connely,' the girl said as the silver half-moon drifted among the stars and the cold desert night settled over us. 'Trish — I'm always called Trish. My father and a handful of his friends and their families were among the first into Canoga Valley. There is a lot of water that seeps from the underground spring in the area, enough to let the long grass grow and feed a dozen small rills. There are a few small bands of Yavapai Indians in the area, but they prefer the highlands to the flats and my father and the others had made friends with them on a previous expedition, and if they did not welcome us exactly, still we kept a respectful distance from each other and have never had a serious incident between white and red man.'

'This was our fifth year on the

Canoga . . . what do I call you?' Trish asked me.

'Giles.'

'This was our fifth year on the Canoga, Giles. We had our houses built and the men had driven in a small herd of shorthorn cattle from California to stock the valley. A few of the ranchers — Gus Staley and Harold Kendrick — had began to plant alfalfa for hay. We were prospering. No one is wealthy along the Canoga, you understand, but we counted ourselves lucky. A thousand square miles of open land, water, almost no Indian troubles.'

Trish fell silent, and so I prompted her. 'And then?'

'And then men began to arrive. They mostly just sat and surveyed the land, watching us at work. No one knew who they were, what they wanted. Until one day the traitor arrived at our ranch.'

'The traitor?' I echoed.

'That's right. He was just a boy, a very sad looking young man with straw-colored hair. His name was Brad

Champion.' Watching Trish's eyes, I had the idea that the young man, whoever he was, had impressed her more than a little. 'We sort of . . . we went out walking a few times,' Trish told me, 'and one night he came to our house. Barney Webb was there, Wes King — I don't know why I'm reeling off the names of people you can't possibly know,' she apologized. 'But the men sat around the table with the lantern glowing low and Brad confessed. He and the other strangers we had noticed were spies for a man named Hammond Cole — sorry, another name you could not know.'

'Could I not?' I mumbled and Trish eyed me narrowly before going on.

'Cole, so Brad told us, was a disaffected Southerner. In his mind the Yankees had taken his family's property in Georgia from him, destroyed his land and way of life after the war. He believed that he had every right to exact payment from the Federal government in return.'

'Canoga Valley?'

'Exactly,' Trish replied. I was shivering and wished for a fire. That, of course, was totally impossible on this secret night.

Trish continued. 'Brad told us all that Cole had conceived a plan to rob us of our land. It went something like this: territorial land being under the control of the US Army, Cole would become their representative. With twenty or thirty men dressed as soldiers, they would enter the valley and produce some sort of document claiming that the land had been illegally settled and that martial law had been declared until the dispute could be resolved. Who would know that this was not an army unit? Who would take arms against them?'

'No one,' I answered. I was beginning to understand the situation and have a glimmer of Hammond Cole's peculiarly warped genius. 'I wonder where he got the uniforms, the horses, the other army gear.'

'Brad thought that they had connections with someone in the quartermaster unit, someone eager to make more money than he could ever acquire on army pay . . . ' She paused. 'Or, we considered, they had simply ambushed a regular army supply train and killed them all.'

I was silent. Was Cole capable of the one and not the other? I recalled his stormy temper and those fierce black eyes. I decided he was capable of either.

'Then what was supposed to happen? According to Brad.'

'After we were driven off the land — along with at least one band of Yavapai Indian — the land was to be turned over, 'sold' at auction to a new group of settlers. Really a gang of toughs led by a man named Shockley — another name that means nothing to you, I'm sure.

'Once they were in place, protected by an army garrison, the men who had acted as soldiers were to drift slowly away, discard their uniforms and one by one return to the Canoga to claim their own sections of land.'

'It's the most audacious plan I have ever heard,' I said. 'Trish, after Brad Champion revealed the scheme, didn't the men of Canoga forge a plan to prevent the land grab?'

'They might have,' she said in a small voice. 'If everyone had believed Brad. If they were willing to take up arms against the US Army. Would you be eager to do that, Giles?' I shook my head negatively. 'Nor were they and three days later — '

I could see the mist in her eyes even by the poor light of the faltering moon.

'Three days later they found Brad dead in a canyon. They tell me he was shot fifteen times . . . I did not count them. I could not look at his young body, riddled as it was.'

After a minute, I asked, 'Who gunned him down, Trish? Who killed Brad Champion?'

'I don't know! It was assumed that he had been shot by those other strangers, for having broken the code of silence.'

She hesitated fractionally. 'Other people thought that it could have been one of us! Someone in cahoots with Cole, perhaps a small landholder drawn by a promise of more land. It was even said that the Indians did it, but no one really believed that. There seemed to be no motive — the Yavapai knew nothing of any of this — and besides Brad's horse was left to stand where it was.'

'Very unlikely that it was them,' I agreed. 'They would have taken the horse. Besides, I can't see an Indian wasting fifteen shots to kill a man when one would do the job, ammunition being as hard to come by as it is out here.'

'But everyone suddenly became mistrustful of neighbors, of the Yavapai, any stranger was looked at with suspicion. And Brad — '

'Did you love him, Trish?' I had to ask.

'Oh, I don't know!' she said in frustration. 'He was honest, he was polite. He seemed to be trying to do the right thing in this world by telling us about Cole. We went out walking a few times. He stole a few kisses from me. Maybe it was only what they call puppy love. But he was young . . . and decent,' she told me. 'I might have loved him after a time. He just didn't deserve to be murdered, Giles. He was only twenty years old.'

'What was it that you and your father had in mind?' I asked, pressing on not because I wished to bring up painful memories, but because I had to understand this all.

'What? If no one else believed Brad, my father did. In an attempt to head the land grab off before it could begin, Father intended to ride to Camp Grant and talk to the army. If all of this about our claims being vacated was true, he wanted to be told in person. If it was a lie, we wanted the cavalry — the real cavalry — there to put a halt to it.'

'Unfortunately,' she said, her eyes now wandering to the hummock where her father lay, 'we achieved nothing in the end.'

I waited, but she said nothing else. I watched as she bowed her head and cried. I stood and took the blanket from under me, walking to Trish to place it over her shoulders as the night's cold grew bitter. I let my hand briefly brush her shoulder and made her a promise so flimsy that it was nearly a lie.

'I'll help you out of this, Trish. I won't let it happen.'

If ever a more meaningless promise has been made, I don't know when. What could I possibly do against the massed army of land grabbers? It was a lie, essentially, that I made to her, but it seemed to give Trish a small measure of comfort to know that she was not alone in her struggle.

We slept.

I don't know how; the night was cold and we were hunted people. Sheer exhaustion and my own deprived body's state demanded it, and so we did sleep, rising near to dawn with a prettily painted sky which would have entertained someone who had no deep concerns to attend to. We, downhearted and shabby, found no pleasure in the garish palette of sunrise.

'We have not discussed it,' Trish said as we recovered the cranky bay and saddled him, 'are you going to take me to Camp Grant?'

'No, Trish,' I said, still holding my saddle. 'We haven't the resources. Were we to reach the army post we would have to convince them of what you were saying. Then it would take the time for them to obtain authorization for such an expedition, the time taken to ride back to Canoga. It could take days or even weeks, and by then Cole and his crew would have already established themselves. They have only to tell their story — the first settlers abandoned their homesteads and they have settled there. What could the army actually do?'

'But then, Giles . . . !'

'But then, there is only one solution.

These men you spoke of — Staley, Kendrick — I can't remember all their names, they must be persuaded to fight for their land. The Yavapai can't be counted on; their people have never profited by fighting the army.'

'Cole has many more men than we do,' Trish argued.

'Yes. Yes, he does. It will depend on who has the better strategy, and on who wants the land more — your people or the intruders.'

'It will be nothing more or less than a range war!'

'Nothing more or less. But,' I said, tightening the cinches on the bay's saddle, 'if they do not care enough for their land to fight for it, then perhaps they don't deserve to hold it.'

Was I talking sense or just talking? I don't know. Maybe it was false bravado manufactured to impress this tiny young woman, but I believed I was right.

'You had better have this, Giles,' she said, handing me a gunbelt with a slick

Colt .44 riding on it. 'It was Father's. I couldn't get it cinched up tight enough to fit me.' I took it thankfully, checking the loads after belting the pistol on. With its comforting weight hanging on my hip I felt almost whole again.

We rode out with the sun still low on the horizon, Trish's arms around my waist. The bay was balky, weary with the miles it had traveled, but the going was easier now despite the double weight it carried. We rode gradually higher and closer to the mountains to the north. The land changed but little. The sun was still a blazing white-hot disc, although a few sheer clouds had appeared, casting thin shadows across the wide land. We had barely enough water remaining in the canteen to swab the horse's mouth from time to time, and soon that was gone.

There being no choice, we made camp at mid-morning beside an acre-sized patch of nopal cactus. Swinging down, Trish asked me why we had halted there.

'The cactus pads. I've seen longhorn steers eat them with the spines on. But we'll start a small fire and burn them off. When they're cooled, they'll make rough forage for the horse. There's plenty of moisture inside.'

And for us, I took a stick and began knocking off the bright red *nopalitos*, the thorny fruit of the cactus. Roasted, peeled, they would provide us with some nourishment as well. As we sat around the fire, toasting these while the bay horse munched on the cactus pads, Trish looked up at me and said:

'You are a funny-looking man.'

I didn't know what to say. Thin shadows from the high, smoky clouds drifted past.

'Did you hear me?' she asked, taking a bite from the seedy, peeled cactus fruit she had been eating.

'Yes, I just don't know what you mean, I suppose.'

'You just are funny-looking, Giles. Look at you! Your eyes don't match for one thing. One of them is kinda green,

76

the other kinda blue-gray. Your hair is almost red, but the sun has bleached it yellow at the ends where it curls over your collar. That blue shirt is definitely the wrong color for you.'

'Anything else?' I asked. At least, I considered, the girl was paying attention to me.

'Yes. You're kinda skinny, but your shoulders bulge out with muscle. And,' she commented as she swallowed, 'your feet's too big.'

'These aren't my boots,' I told her grouchily. 'Anything else you're in the mood to criticize?'

'No,' she shook her head, 'Outside of your nose which is kinda twisted, you're a fine-looking specimen.'

I just looked skyward, holding my tongue. I wondered if that was the weakest compliment a man could ever have received from a girl: 'Fine-looking specimen.'

A question had been on my mind for some time and now, since we had descended to a personal level, it seemed a good time to ask her:

'How old are you, Trish?'

'Why?' the question seemed to offend her. 'I am nineteen and one-half years old. If you are going to say that I look younger — I have heard that all my life.'

'I wasn't going to say anything. I just have sort of wondered.'

'Well, don't say anything, if you please,' she said huffily and then rose to her feet turning her back on me.

'How far is it to Canoga?' I asked, changing the subject.

'Twenty miles, at a guess.'

'We're still well ahead of Hammond Cole and his army, then. I'd like to rest the horse, but I can't walk just yet, and — '

'I'll walk alongside,' Trish said. 'Don't object out of some misplaced sense of chivalry!' she added, lifting a hand to still my protest. 'I can walk; you can't. The solution is obvious.'

We started on, me on the plodding bay, the little girl with the wild frizzy hair marching determinedly beside me, the Spencer .56 repeater on her shoulder. In the white light of the desert day her hair seemed almost white. Her eyes, I had learned, were deep blue. I had tied my bandanna over my head pirate-style, but it did little to keep the searing heat from my skull and its jumbled contents. There was little time to talk. The super-heated air made it difficult to breathe, and Trish, eager though she was to prove that she was a tough little woman, was faltering, her stride shortening. More than once I offered to switch places with her, but after her third firm refusal I didn't bring it up again.

'What are you doing out here, Giles?' she did ask once as I let the horse pause to blow. We had halted on a low barren rise where the ubiquitous black volcanic rock was strewn across the ground, memories of some ancient caldera no longer visible. 'No one belongs out here.'

'You're here,' I reminded her.

'You know what we were trying to

do,' Trish said pettishly, 'trying to save our land, our homes.'

I considered my answer for a minute before I shrugged and said simply, 'I had some trouble on my backtrail. There was no choice but to try to escape into the desert.'

'I see,' she said thoughtfully. 'When there's time, will you tell me all about it?'

'Yes. Yes, I will Trish, when there is time.'

But now was not the time for it. We started down the slope, the bay moving tentatively. Above us three vultures circled on fixed black wings, the updraft holding them aloft effortlessly. They had spotted no carrion yet: had they, there would have been a cloud of the scavengers gathering, drawn there by their secret signals.

How much time had we? I remembered hearing the two soldiers talking, back with the wagon train. They had said that they meant to reach Canoga the next afternoon — this afternoon. I didn't know if they knew what they were talking about. It could have had no more weight than barracks chatter, jailhouse rumors. Something leaked to the weary soldiers to bolster their morale.

I could not judge the distances, calculate how much of a lead — if any — we had on the land grabbers. Once in Canoga the settlers would have to be gathered from far-flung ranches, told of the situation. Then, we would have to convince them that the rumor young Brad Champion had carried to them was true. They would have to have enough confidence in their conviction to make them stand up to the US Army.

And then they would have to organize a plan of action. A leader would be needed who could put it into play . . . me? I grimaced at the thought. I was never cut out for a general. Besides I was a wandering man, a stranger unknown to any of the settlers. It all seemed impossible now that I had

had the time to think it through. And if I failed . . .

Well, someone had taught Brad Champion not to interfere. Fifteen bullets. I wondered how long it would take to kill a man like that. Was the first one the one that ended his life, or did the blows of each shot, like the impact of a sledge hammer, allow him to live long enough to feel the terrible jolt of each and every one of them?

'There it is!' Trish said, halting as she pointed into the distances. I could see nothing through the heat-haze at first, and then I did.

A broad valley stretched out in all directions from the foot of a low line of hills. The ground was a gray-green, indicating water and growing grass. I even saw, or imagined I did, a few scattered buildings no larger than dice cubes.

'That's Canoga, Giles,' Trish said, turning to stand next to my saddle, her eyes looking up hopefully. 'Now everything will be all right.'

Would it? I couldn't see how, but I looked into her searching eyes and manufactured a smile for her benefit.

Then we started on down toward the long valley where hard-working people were going about their daily lives, unaware of the war fire hovering over them. I glanced skyward. A dozen other vultures had joined the slowly circling watchers.

5

There was a cluster of a dozen white-faced cattle standing scattered across an unfenced meadow. They looked up with bovine uninterest as we rode along the lane toward the small unpainted house ahead of us. Behind me on the bay, her arms around my waist again, Trish said with an air of apology:

'We were going to whitewash the cabin next week.'

I didn't comment. The house was small, cozy, shaded by a trio of live-oak trees. It was finer than any home I had ever had. Behind the house some fifty feet or so was a barn, also unpainted. I asked hopefully, 'Do you have other horses, Trish?'

'Two, but they'll have to be caught up. We couldn't leave them in the barn while we were gone.'

'No. I'll see to the bay and do what I can do about catching up the other horses. We'll be needing them.'

'What can I do?' Trish asked.

'Spread the word. Can you walk to your nearest neighbor? We've got to get the word out and hold a meeting to figure out what we can do. Trish,' I said, 'they have to be made to understand that it is a choice between fighting or running. If they run they lose everything they have worked for over the past five years. There is no middle ground, no other way.'

By the time I had stabled up the weary bay horse and forked well-deserved hay for it, pumped water into his trough, cooled myself off with the water and returned to the house I found a new Trish Connely there. She was wearing a dark blue dress with tiny dots of white on it and had managed to brush and pin up her frizzy hair using one of those secrets known only to women. It was arranged in a sleek, drawn-back sort of arrangement that flattered her face.

'Did you manage to get the horses caught?' she asked, not turning from the mirror as I entered the small front room of the comfortable-appearing house.

'Not yet. I saw them, though. They looked interested in coming back to see what was happening at the barn. A red roan and a big buckskin — that them?' I asked.

'Yes.'

I had seated myself in a deep red-cushioned chair, and she must have known that I was studying her slender back, for she turned sharply, her cheeks slightly flushed. 'I thought it was a good idea to clean up a little so that I didn't look like a wild-eyed maniac when I went to ask the Webbs for help.'

'They're the nearest neighbors? Is that the Barney Webb you mentioned?'

'Yes, he, his wife and three sons. I don't know if I should tell them what happened on the trail to Camp Grant, about — ' She was remembering her

86

father, I knew. His death seemed pointless in a way, but there was something heroic in the man's attempt to rescue them all from a bad situation.

'I think you should tell them,' I said, rising to my feet. 'Maybe you could embellish a little, tell them that your father wanted them to know that his fears were well-founded.'

'How — ?'

'If you're not above a small white lie, you can say that you and your father talked to me before he died. I corroborated Brad Champion's story.' She listened, mulled it over and nodded with determination.

'That's the way to do it, I suppose. And then — ?'

'Tell them that I want to meet with them all. Here, or at Barney Webb's house — it doesn't matter. But convince them that it must be done hastily. There is no time to wait. The soldiers could arrive at any time, even as early as this afternoon from what I overheard.'

'And what would happen then?' Trish asked uneasily.

I shrugged, I did not really know, but I guessed, 'They declare martial law. Everyone confined to his own home, meetings banned. I don't know, Trish. I just know the settlers have no time to waste if they mean to save their homes.' I paused. 'Maybe I can catch up one of the horses quickly. I hate to see you walk.'

'That would take time, wouldn't it? It's no more than half a mile to the Webb ranch. I can be there before you can rope and saddle one of the ponies.' She tilted her head back and instructed me, 'There is lye soap in the kitchen. You could stand a little slicking-up, too, Giles. I'll be gone. You can wash yourself. Father . . . Father might have a clean shirt in his dresser that will fit you.'

Then she turned, hoisted her skirts and walked out on to the porch, down the steps and out into the sunlight, her back rigidly held, moving determinedly up the road. I watched her until she was lost among the shadows of the oak trees and then went out to try to catch the two horses before cleaning up.

Within half an hour I was standing over the zinc tub in the corner of the kitchen, washing the alkali, dust and dried blood from my body. The horses had been curious about events, as I had told Trish. Having grazed on rough forage for the past few days, drinking little water, they followed me back into the barn as I waved a handful of alfalfa hay under their noses. The roan was friendlier, but the old, stocky buckskin offered no real objection either as I placed them into their stalls, gave each a bucket of water and a forkful of hay and left them to introduce themselves to the bay.

By the time Trish returned, riding on the seat of a surrey driven by a competent-looking ranch woman, I had scrubbed, dressed myself in one of her father's white shirts and brushed most of the tangles out of my hair. I stood on the porch, hands on my hips, watching them arrive in a swirl of light dust. The women were grim-appearing, and well they should be. A choice had to be made: fight for your land, and watch friends or family possibly die, or flee into the wasteland beyond the Canoga Valley without provisions or a promising destination.

I tied up the buggy horse and helped Trish down. The older woman, whom I took to be Mrs. Webb, alighted on her own and stood watching me with a suspicious, frozen expression, as if I were to blame for all of their troubles. They say that that is always the way with a messenger of bad tidings.

We trooped into the house, the women holding their skirts up. Trish talked to me as we entered the small house. 'Grace has sent her three boys out to the other ranches. Barney Webb was plowing his fields and insisted on finishing what he was doing before rushing over here.'

'I understand,' I said, as the two

women seated themselves. And I did. A man busy at work, concentrating on his task, is not eager to store his plow, unhitch his mules and rush over to a hastily called meeting arriving from out of the blue.

'We may as well have coffee — or tea, Mrs Webb — while we are waiting,' Beth said and she went into the kitchen, leaving me alone with the dour Grace Webb.

'We have heard all of this before, you know,' she said to me. 'Warnings, rumors.'

I nodded. 'They're all too true, Mrs. Webb. I can assure you of that. We didn't summon all of you on a whim.'

'It had better not be,' she warned me. 'I left my sugar-cookie dough in a bowl. It'll be hard as a rock if I don't get back to it soon.'

If you ever do, I thought but did not say. Emergencies do not arrive at convenient times.

After one cup of tea hastily sipped, Mrs. Webb rose and announced that she had to be on her way. None of the men had arrived yet, and I wondered if any of those summoned would come at all.

Trish served coffee at the tiny kitchen table and buttered some thickly sliced bread for me. It was a little stale, I suppose, but it was more than I had had in a long time. While we dined, Trish asked me again how I had come to get caught up in all of this.

'I was working on a small ranch near Mesa Grande, the Doubletree, by name. I was yard man and wrangler combined. One day the boss, Jeff Farrel asked me to take his prized black into town to get it re-shod. It seemed like a pleasant way to spend a day away from my chores. I'd just have to drop the horse at the farrier's and while I was waiting, there would be time to drink a beer or two. I was looking forward to the day off.'

'What happened?' Trish asked.

'I took a shortcut up the wrong alley,' I told her and continued on through the long story. When I was finished, Trish asked:

'Why are you risking it — staying here? You know that Hammond Cole will be angry with you. You know that Jake Shockley would not mind having a second chance at hanging you. Why didn't you just take one of my horses and ride away?'

It was a good question. I didn't know. I had no real answer. Perhaps it was that I wanted to see Shockley again when he didn't have the upper hand. Maybe I still hoped to take him back to Mesa Grande to clear my name. Maybe, I considered, the real reason was sitting across the table from me, blue eyes wondering at my actions. I never answered Trish's question. From the front of the house we heard horses arriving in the yard, and we rose to meet the inriders.

Trish introduced the three men as they stepped up on to the porch and entered the small front room. None of them smiled at me, and only the narrowly-built Harold Kendrick shook my hand, and that briefly.

'Now what is all of this?' Barney Webb asked. He sat heavily on the sofa, his weight bowing the yellow cushion. He was irritable, balding and missing two front teeth. 'Trish, so help me, if this is more of the same spook story that that Brad Champion was going on about — '

'I'm afraid it is, Barney,' Trish said. He sighed deeply, muttering, 'Wes King was right to keep to his work.'

'This man,' Trish said, indicating me, 'was with the phony army of land grabbers that Brad Champion was trying to warn us all about. He can tell you what he saw, what he heard. Please! Take a minute to listen. It's dreadfully important.'

'Is it?' the blustering rancher asked.

I replied, 'Only if you want to keep your house and your land.'

Gus Staley, a nervous, ineffectual-looking man with pale watery eyes spoke up, 'We can at least listen, Barney.'

'We've ridden over here,' Kendrick agreed. 'Let's at least hear what he has to say.'

I told them. Told them how I knew that the soldiers were not real cavalrymen, that Cole could not be much more than a day behind us, maybe not that much. I told them about the Shockley gang and their intention to hold the land. Barney Webb seemed only bored by this repetition of Brad Champion's warnings. Harold Kendrick listened thoughtfully, nodding his head now and then, his eyes turned to the carpet. Gus Staley's face was intent, his watery eyes reflecting uncertainty and fear.

'Are you positive they are not the real army?' he asked without lifting his eyes.

'Yes.'

'You couldn't know that, unless you were among them — but you say that you were,' Webb said with suspicion.

'Not voluntarily.'

'So you say. Look here, men,' Barney Webb went on. 'If this is a regular cavalry force riding this way, we can't take up arms against them. If they are impostors — how many men, Clanahan?'

'Twenty, thirty.'

'Then I don't see how we could do anything to stop them either. There's not more than a dozen able-bodied men on the Canoga, and for the most part we're farmers, poor ranchers, not soldiers.'

'Maybe we should just pull out until they've come and gone,' Kendrick suggested weakly. 'They can't stay here forever, can they?'

'Weren't you listening!' big Barney Webb said, nearly shouting. 'If Clanahan's story is true — which I doubt — there is already another band of men set to arrive once we've been driven off. Then the so-called army splits up, loses their uniforms and returns to divvy up the rest of our land. Isn't that what you claim, Clanahan?'

'That's it, yes.'

'We don't have a chance,' Gus Staley said.

'We wouldn't, no — not if any of what he's saying is true. I just don't happen to believe that it is. For myself,' Webb said, rising heavily, putting his hat on, 'I'm going to sit it out and wait. No ghosts are going to run me off of my land. If the time comes when I have to fight — well, then I will.'

'It will be too late by then,' I said.

'If any of what you're saying is true,' Webb said, 'it's already too late, isn't it.' Then he deliberately turned his back on us and stalked out the door, leaving it open so that the harsh afternoon sunlight glared in, painting a yellow rectangle on the floor of the small house. The other two men had risen, but their movements were more indefinite.

'What was it that you had in mind, Clanahan,' Gus Staley asked, turning his hat in his hands, 'about fighting these men off?'

'That is the thing,' I told him

97

honestly. 'I don't know this area at all. I wanted to have a meeting to see who was able, who was willing and who would help me devise a plan of action.'

'You must have had a lot of experience as a soldier sometime,' Staley said. There was no point in lying.

'I never served a day.'

His eyes which had begun to grow hopeful as we spoke now seemed to darken. He put his hat on and gestured to Kendrick. The two walked slowly toward the door. Staley paused to say, 'We'll have to consider this further, Clanahan. Talk among ourselves. It's a risky thing you're proposing.'

'It's riskier to wait,' I said.

Without another word the two men went out, swung into their saddles and turned their horses from the yard. Trish touched my elbow as I stood watching them go, and I looked down at her.

'They're not cowards, Giles. They're just confused.' She smiled bitterly. 'I wish you'd have lied and told them what a great career you'd had as a solider.'

'It wouldn't have done any good. They'll believe me only when it's too late.'

We went back into the house. I helped Trish clean up the mess in the kitchen, performing the task in silence. I was placing the last dried dish up on the shelf when we heard horses arriving. Trish bolted toward the door and I followed, my hand on my pistol butt.

'Who is it?' I asked, peering at the new arrivals through the swirl of dust they had sent skyward as they reined up.

'Barney Webb's sons,' Trish told me and we stood back to allow the three blond young men, all alike as to features and build, enter the house. Each removed his hat as he came in. I guessed their ages at between sixteen and nineteen. The youngest, the one his brother called Ned, might have been even younger. There was a sense of urgency about them and they refused a seat and instead stood standing in a half-circle, hats in hand.

'I'm Charles Webb,' the oldest boy said. 'These are my brothers — Oliver and Ned. We've come to help.'

I looked at the three eager, grim faces and shook my head, glancing at Trish. 'Thanks, men, but — '

'But we're too young!' Charles Webb said with some antagonism. He tossed his hat on the sofa and seated himself. Folding his hands between his knees he looked up at me and said, 'If something isn't done, we've had it, isn't that right? Look, Brad Champion was a friend to all of us. He wasn't here long, but we all talked to him and knew he was dead serious even if the old men didn't think so.' He held up a hand to keep me from interrupting. 'There's more. We passed Gus Staley and Harold Kendrick on our way over. They were still talking. I think they're leaning toward helping too, but they want to talk to the others, those who couldn't make it over here today. Our father and Wes King won't do anything until their land is pulled out from under them. There's a couple other young guys around who might want to help — I can't speak for everybody, but my brothers and I are here, and we won't wait for the other men to make up their minds,' he finished, his eyes hot with the impetuousness of youth.

'What can we do?' Ollie Webb asked. The same determination was in his eyes.

I sighed, rubbed my forehead. Shrugged. What could I tell them after pleading urgency to their father and his friends? Things were urgent, I knew that, and it seemed that they realized it as well. 'Let's sit down to the kitchen table,' I said finally. 'I need to know something about the lay of the land, maybe you can put together a rough sketch for me so that I can have some understanding of it. Charles, I want you to ride to Camp Grant and tell them — '

'No sir!' the eldest brother said

firmly. 'Send the kid.' He nodded at his brother who was no more than two or three years younger than he.

'All right,' I agreed. 'This is no time to argue. Ned, then: take two horses so you can switch off from time to time, and make sure to carry waterbags.' Trish interrupted to make sure that Ned knew about the poison waterhole. Then she asked me a question: 'Giles, you said that the army would delay forever making up their minds.'

'That was when we had only a warning of attack. Ned,' I said, speaking carefully to the youngest Webb boy. 'You are to tell them that we are under attack by raiders and things are desperate. Nothing more. Do you understand me?'

'I do,' Ned replied with the same determination his older brothers showed.

'How long do you think it will take you to reach the camp?'

'If I leave now and ride hard, I can make it by midnight,' Ned replied.

'Then scoot! We're all depending on you.'

He was out the door without another word, turning his pony sharply on its heels as he spurred it out of the yard. To the two older boys I said, 'Now, then. I want you to help me with a battle plan. After that's done, I want you to ride to the outlying ranches and see if anyone else is willing to join us. We won't count on Staley, Kendrick, and their hands to join us until we see them coming.'

Half an hour later both of the Webb boys had left the ranch as well, heading in opposite directions. I watched them until the dust settled.

Trish had said not a word for the last fifteen minutes as the Webbs sat drawing a map of the Canoga for me to study. Now, bringing me a mug of steaming coffee, she said, 'What are you thinking, Giles?'

'I'm thinking that I wish to hell that I was a man who *had* had a great deal of military experience. Frankly, this not only worries me, it scares me. I don't like being responsible for those young men — for any of them.'

'You'll do fine,' Trish said warmly.

I almost believed her.

'You've given everyone orders except me,' Trish commented, fixing her dark blue eyes on me. 'What do you want me to do, Giles?'

'Saddle a horse and ride. Get out of here, Trish. There will be too many guns and too much blood. I don't want you here.'

'Uh-uh,' she responded. 'No, Giles. You asked everyone else to stay and fight for their land. Why should I be the exception? I'm willing to fight, too. I owe it to my father's memory. I'm in this with you to the bitter end.'

6

We could see their dust. Studying them through the field glasses that Charles Webb had brought along, I could make out the horses, small as ants and the wagons they were pulling. Hammond Cole's soldiers, flanked out on either side of the trail, moved slowly toward Canoga, their horses obviously desert-weary.

'I counted twenty-two men,' Charles said as I handed the binoculars back to him. His expression was grim but not fearful. He passed the field glasses to his brother, Oliver, who lay stretched out beside us as we studied the approaching enemy from the sun-heated ledge of stone. Below us was the road Cole must travel to reach the Canoga. I had noted that when first studying the map the Webb boys had drawn up for me.

There were only two ways to reach Canoga, sheltered as it was on three sides by the broken hills. The first was across the naked desert, the route Trish and I had traveled; the second was up through the depths of the mile-long canyon. This was the trail the settlers used when they had to leave Canoga to conduct business or reach far-off Tucson to freight in supplies. Cole's spies had certainly reported this to him after reconnoitering the valley.

'How are we going to fight that many!' Ollie asked with a soft whistle.

'Maybe Dad and the others will believe us now and get together,' Charles said. He looked hopefully to me. 'Giles?'

'We can only delay them,' I said. 'Try to hold them back until the cavalry from Fort Grant can reach us — or at least until the ranchers can arm themselves for the fight.'

'Delay them?' Charles's face was blank, then as he peered down the long red-walled canyon the hint of a smile appeared. 'Oh . . . I see!'

'Somebody tell me,' Ollie Webb said heatedly. 'I don't know what you two have in mind.'

A part of the solution, although only a temporary one loomed beside and above us, an upthrusting monument of crumbling red rocks. Some of the stones were house-sized — these we could not hope to move without explosives, but others seemed so precariously balanced that with effort and the help of inertia, they could be sent rolling and tumbling from the canyon rim. Would this be enough to clog the road making passage impossible? Probably not, but certainly enough to halt the wagons, enough to make picking one's way through on horseback slow and dangerous. Dangerous because once the landslide occurred the riders would become aware that there were men watching them through their gunsights from the rim above.

'Pa would kill us,' Ollie said dolefully. 'You know how long it took to grade that road in the first place?'

Charles and I ignored the complaint. For his part Charles was already to his feet, circling the towering stack of boulders, searching for a weak spot.

'That won't stop them, if they're as determined as you say,' Ollie complained. 'After we block the trail — supposing we can — they'll still be able to ride their horses through or around, won't they?' Sweat trickled from his forehead into his eyes.

'Then we'll be waiting to slow them down,' I said. 'With snipers up here, they won't be eager to advance. After dark Cole may try it . . . but I wouldn't want to ride that road in the dark.'

'They can go around,' Ollie pointed out, 'circle back to the desert and ride in the back side of the valley — like you did.'

'They can,' I was forced to agree, 'but that takes time, at least an entire day. Nothing we do can hold Cole back forever, but if this works, it may delay them long enough so that the soldiers from Camp Grant will have time to get here.'

'You say that as if you're sure they'll come. That they'll listen to Ned, believe some kid with a wild story, drop what they're doing and come to our rescue.' Ollie, I thought, was close to tears despite his nearness to manhood.

'You see that outcropping just above where that broken piñon is rooted,' Charlie Webb was saying as he strode up to us, dusting his jeans off. 'The rocks underneath are ready to crumble away. It wouldn't take much to get them rolling. Then, if the ledge follows, we can make us a hell of a mess down below.'

'All right,' I agreed, 'let's give it a try.' Charlie was grinning, relishing the idea of starting a landslide to block off the road below. Ollie just looked miserable.

Hammond Cole's 'cavalry' was still far distant. The men were without recognizable features, the horses all the same shadowy color as they neared the mouth of the canyon where it fanned out on to the long sage-studded desert flats.

'Maybe we should fire a few warning shots,' Ollie suggested.

'It'd be like throwing peas at them, Ollie. I doubt they'd even hear the reports. Wait. There'll be plenty of time to shoot later.'

He nodded mutely, standing there with his Winchester in hand, obviously stunned by the situation he had gotten himself into. Charles meanwhile had clambered up on to the face of the column of crumbling red stone and cinched his rope around the most likely looking one of the bunch — the keystone, or so we hoped. Returning, he played out his lariat and swung into his horse's saddle, throwing a dally loop around his pommel.

'Here goes nothing,' he said cheerfully and he began backing his pony from the crumbling monument. I found myself holding my breath as the rope drew taut and the little chestnut horse braced itself with all four feet and struggled against the strain of the rope. I saw — thought I saw — some of the smaller, head-sized stones beneath and beside the boulder move as the horse continued to back. Charlie's face was set grimly as he urged the horse to continue.

When the slide began it was nothing like I had imagined. A dozen rocks the size of a kid's ball trickled from beneath the boulder Charlie had lashed on to and tumbled over the rim, rolling and bouncing down the canyon walls. A trickle of red dust followed. Then the whole pile of rotten sandstone seemed to come apart at once as if someone had set off a dynamite charge.

'Slip the line, Charlie!' I yelled, and he looked at me blankly. Then his eyes opened wide as he saw the entire upper table of stone dip its head and cut loose. He managed to slip the dally knot and fling the rope aside as the boulder he had been tugging on jerked to one side, hesitated and then racketed down the canyon, splitting in two as it went. The rest of the red ledge followed and a mountain of stone, hundreds of tons of it, followed it into the maw of the canyon, sending clouds of red dust skyward.

Ollie and I stood on the lip of the canyon rim, watching in awe as the mass of bounding, rolling, sliding stone thundered into its depths. Charlie slipped up beside us and croaked dryly: 'If I'd been a few seconds slower. Me and my pony both — '

I gripped his shoulder and grinned. 'You weren't, though.'

We watched the rocks thunder downward, and through the veil of settling dust we could see that there was no way a wagon would pass that way; it would be tricky for a man on horseback, and once they knew there were snipers up there, they would soon give that up as well.

'You did it, Charlie,' I said appreciatively and he grinned.

'I guess I did,' he replied. 'But, Giles

— don't ever let me pull such a fool stunt again!'

The wind had begun to fuss a little and the fine red dust drifted southward. We could see that the soldiers had pulled up. There was some kind of activity among them, ant-sized horsemen moving in confused circles.

'Somebody's got to go back to Trish's place and tell them what has happened. Find out if any more men have stepped forward to volunteer to help us,' I said.

'That's a job for you, Giles,' Ollie replied.

'I guess it is,' I said, although I still hated to leave these two young men out here on their own. 'Is there another way around?' I asked Charles. 'Or have we got them blocked for now?'

'There's an old Indian trail,' he said, nodding toward the west. 'But I doubt that even their spies found it. Besides, we can see anyone trying to loop that way.'

'Not after dark,' I commented, looking to the skies which were beginning to dull and color with the approach of sunset.

'After dark I don't think anyone can travel that road,' Charlie said. 'It was meant to be a footpath only. I wouldn't want to take a horse up or down it even in daylight.'

'All right, then,' I said. 'If they get within reasonable rifle range, you might want to pepper them with a few warning shots. It would be a miracle if you hit anything, but it will give them the idea. Just don't burn up ammo needlessly.'

I swung into the saddle of Trish's buckskin horse. I had chosen the ornery cuss over the placid roan because he seemed tough and toughness was what I figured to require of a horse before this was ended.

I followed the same trail the boys had shown me back to the settlement. I didn't know the area well enough to take a chance on another route. The breeze was drifting through the upper reaches of the gnarled piñon pine trees

I passed through as I circled the upper limit of the canyon and reached the wagon road into Canoga. For the first mile the land was rocky, studded with yucca and tightly growing manzanita in the washes, but eventually I reached the flats where the ground water encouraged buffalo grass and wild oats to grow. I saw them coming before they could have seen me with the ball of the low red sun at my back and I drew up, waiting cautiously.

When they were nearer enough to recognize I lifted a hand and called out. Gus Staley and Harold Kendrick, wearing coats, carrying rifles, reined in alongside me.

'Where you fellows riding to?' I asked.

'We figured you could use some help out here,' Kendrick said.

'We could. How'd you know there was trouble?'

'Couldn't miss that,' Kendrick said, waving an arm toward the southern sky where traces of the red cloud the landslide had caused still hung in the evening air.

'I appreciate your coming,' I said honestly. 'I didn't feel too good about leaving the two Webb boys back there on their own. They figured that it was up to me to return to Canoga and see if I could muster some more men.'

'I doubt that will happen,' Kendrick said, turning his head to spit. 'Barney Webb will likely be looking to bash your head in for you.'

'Why?' I asked in surprise.

'You sent his three boys off. He wants those boys at home, working from dawn to dusk, not off playing soldier.'

'I didn't force them to come along,' I said. 'They just seemed to have a better understanding of circumstances than their father.'

'Barney's plumb mean when he's mad,' Gus Staley said.

'That can't be helped. I'm trying to save his land for him, for all of you. I'm not getting much in the way of thanks.'

'Why?' Staley asked laconically. 'Why

are you doing it, Clanahan?'

'You know why, Gus,' Harold Kendrick said with a faint smile. I knew they were referring to Trish, but chose to ignore the implication.

I went on: 'If Barney Webb would take the trouble to ride out here, I could show him the proof of what we've been saying. We've an army of land grabbers cut off in the canyon.'

'That wouldn't matter to Webb. He doesn't believe anything he doesn't want to,' Kendrick said. 'Harold and me got to talking about matters after we left Trish Connely's house. It was Webb and Wes King who got us to disbelieving that young fellow, Brad Champion, when he warned us. Well, we figured that maybe Barney was right back then. But when a second man comes to tell the same tale, you've got to rearrange your thinking some.'

'There's a few of the other men who are leaning the same way,' Gus Staley said. 'Think we can hold off this so-called army if we all were to get together?'

'I don't know,' I admitted. 'But it beats loading your wagons and pulling off the land without a fight, doesn't it?' The buckskin horse shifted its feet impatiently under me. The land was purpling, darkness settling rapidly. 'I'd better let you boys go along,' I said, 'but before you do, tell me: what in the hell is the matter with Barney Webb?'

'Want me to tell him, Gus? It's like this,' Harold Kendrick said, leaning forward in the saddle, his hands crossed on the pommel. 'Barney Webb and Wes King were late-comers to Canoga. The rest of us had been living on our homesteads for almost a year. There really wasn't any land worth a damn that hadn't been filed on already.'

'Barney Webb had a wife and three boys with him and we figured, well — we've been lucky to find this valley, and these folks have nothing. We told Webb and King that we would be willing to shave a little off our property so that they could try to make a start up here. Told them, though, that it wasn't going to be the best land, the easiest to till or having the best water.'

Kendrick went on. 'They shook our hands, said that it was big of us, that whatever we could work out they would be satisfied and grateful.'

'They ain't been neither one since,' Gus Staley grumbled.

'I see,' I said thoughtfully, wondering at the implications of what I had heard. The wind was cool on my back now and the trail was darkening rapidly.

'We'd better be going now, Clanahan. Take some well-meant advice. Watch yourself around Barney Webb. And Wes King.'

'Did you give Brad Champion the same advice?' I asked, and they looked through me, not at me before they started their ponies ahead, following the canyon trail up toward the piney ridge.

I rode past three or four small ranches as the sky went to blue-black and the stars began to blink on. Within a mile of Trish's house I came across three more men riding west. Their leader was a rough-looking, whiskered man named DeFord, a lanky scarecrow of a rancher called Dee Cobbold and a third man who never offered his name.

'After listening to Gus Staley and Kendrick, we figured it was time to help out,' DeFord told me as the four of us briefly reined up at the side of the road. 'There's a few more men waiting at the Connely ranch to talk to you. Nobody really knows what to do, but there's more of us willing to try whatever it takes.'

That lifted my spirits some. As I approached Trish's house, I could see that DeFord had been telling the truth. Not a few horses, but as many as ten stood tethered to the hitchrail and beneath the oak trees. I rode directly to the house, swung down and started toward the door without seeing to my horse first. Something I never did, but these were extraordinary times. The door was closed, but it swung open as I stepped up on to the porch.

The first man I saw, framed in the

doorway, his thick features twisted with anger, was Barney Webb.

'Webb — ' I began, but he didn't want to hear what I had to tell him.

'You rotten bastard!' he bellowed. 'What are you trying to do to me? Sneaking around behind my back and dragging my three sons into your problems?'

I would have told him, but never got the chance. With his last words, Webb stepped out to meet me and I saw his heavy fist arcing through the air but could not duck quickly enough to get out of its way. His blow struck against the side of my skull, a glancing strike above my ear. It wasn't enough to take me down, but plenty enough to start my head spinning. There were colored pin-wheels behind my eyes as I crouched, raised my hands in front of my face to ward him off and stepped back away from his onslaught. Webb wasn't finished with me yet. He had only begun.

I backed into a pole upright and took a heavy blow to my ribs. Cursing, I jabbed back with my left, trying to get the hulking rancher off of me. I did manage to slip one good shot in past his raised fists and saw with satisfaction that I had cracked his nose hard enough to start the blood flowing from his nostrils. That didn't slow him down either, but only enraged him further. I tried to back away as I continued to jab at the big man's face, but my bootheel hit the edge of the porch and I tripped, stumbling into the yard where the light from within the cabin lit a patch of earth about the side of a prize-fighting ring. Behind Webb now I could see a crowd of men gathered, a few of them cheering him on, others watching soberly.

Webb came at me steadily, plodding ahead, winging lefts and rights, some of which I was able to block, some of which landed on my shoulders, head and neck with stunning force. Continuing to back away I jabbed sharply, looping one right-hand shot over his guard to land above his left eye. It did little damage and did nothing to slow him down.

He swung at me again, missing, and I kicked him on the kneecap as hard as I could. Groaning, Webb staggered slightly, involuntarily bent forward to clutch his damaged knee and I swung an upper-cut with everything I had in me, catching him on the point of his shovel-shaped jaw. It felt like I had shattered every bone in my hand, but Webb got even worse. His eyes rolled up in his head, his arms went limp and he stood there bobbing apelike for a moment before falling forward to land on his face against the hard-packed earth of the ranch yard.

Panting I leaned over him, fists still clenched, but he did not rise or even twitch. Rubbing my right hand, I stepped over him and returned to the porch. No one said anything, no one tried to stop me as I entered the house, looked around . . .

And saw Jake Shockley sitting in Trish's chair, studying me with glittering, hate-filled eyes.

7

The moment was incomprehensible. I thought I must have taken one too many punches. There, in Trish's living room sat Jake Shockley, and standing around the room I recognized Curt and the man called Vallejo from Campo del Bianca, among the other tough-looking strangers.

'They say that it's a small world, don't they, Clanahan?' Shockley said. 'This is the man who killed me, boys. The way he keeps following me, it seems he wants to try it again. Some people are just plain crazy.'

Behind me I heard heavy, shuffling steps and glanced toward the door to see Barney Webb, battered more than I had thought, enter, blood smeared across his face. His eyes lit hungrily and he started toward me, hands balling into fists.

'Sit down, Webb!' Jake Shockley commanded. 'You had your chance.'

Only now as I glanced around the room again, did I see young Ned Webb standing in a far corner, his head bowed. He looked up now and waved a hand limply. 'I'm sorry, Clanahan. I rode right into them before I knew who they were.'

'It's all right, Ned,' I told him.

So the army had not been alerted to the trouble on the Canoga. Where did that leave us, I wondered. The ranchers I had met all seemed to be capable men in their way, but they would be no match for the gang of thugs riding with Jake Shockley. I knew now why Barney Webb had been so angry — it wasn't that I had taken his sons from their work or enlisted them to fight, it was that I had dispatched Ned to Fort Grant, carrying a message that could have destroyed all of their plans.

'I suppose,' I said to Shockley, 'that these are the new settlers.'

He came as close to a smile as he

could. 'That's right. The only thing is, you've kind of snarled things up. We haven't yet gotten the army to evict the old settlers.' His hands came together and clenched tightly. 'This could have all been done nice and neat, Clanahan, but you had to get involved in something that's none of your business. Now there's no way the original plan will work. Now, it seems, there are a lot of people who are going to be killed. We can't let anyone ride off to tell the tale, can we? And it's all your fault for meddling, Clanahan. Live with that if you can.' He paused and lifted those dark eyes to meet mine.

'Not that you'll be alive that much longer yourself.'

I had already figured as much, and Shockley's pronouncement didn't rock me as much as he intended it to. I knew what the odds on my living were. They sometimes say 'between slim and none', but I didn't figure my chances even rose to the level of slim. I had another, more urgent thought buzzing in my skull, and if Shockley thought he saw panic in my eyes, maybe he did because of it:

Where was Trish?

'You can't get away with it, you know,' I said.

'With what?' Shockley asked with mock surprise. 'By the time the army, anyone else gets up here to investigate we'll have a sad tale to tell of an Indian uprising.'

'The Yavapai! Don't make me laugh, Shockley. They're not a hostile people.'

'Nobody will know what band of Indians did it — Apaches, maybe — we just came along and found the unhappy result. Men killed, tortured . . . '

'Women and children?' I persisted, glancing at Barney Webb and the tall man standing beside him, who I took to be Wes King. Shockley didn't answer. 'Well, you'd have to kill them too, wouldn't you? If even one person were left alive to tell the tale you'd lose everything. Did you think about that, Webb, when you signed this pact with the devil? What about your sons? Your wife. *You*, come to think of it. Why, you'd have something to hold over Jake's head the rest of his life, wouldn't you?'

'Why don't you shut up, Clanahan,' Jake Shockley said. 'Barney knows I treat my friends right. He's got first choice of the property when we start carving it up. No more trying to scratch a living on that dust patch the settlers gave him.'

Barney Webb was wavering, but he could not afford to do so. He was in the game to the limit, all of his chips on the table. He *had* to believe Jake Shockley.

'Cole might not like this,' I said, and Jake's stolid face for once showed surprise.

'You know Hammond Cole?' he demanded, half-rising.

'We've met. I traveled a way with him.'

Shockley sagged back into the chair, looking deeply thoughtful. 'Did he have — ?' His question broke off and he wagged his head heavily. 'Not now,' he decided. 'Get him out of here,' Jake said, pointing a finger at me. 'I don't have time to fool with him. There's too much to do.' Again he formed that mirthless smile and told me, 'You'll keep. I just have to decide which tree is the right one to hang you from.'

'Why don't you just shoot him!' Barney Webb demanded. His eyes had a fiery hatred in them that had not been there before. I must have stirred up his emotions with my little speech.

'I have a few more questions for Clanahan,' Shockley answered. 'Besides, I promised him that he'd hang,' Shockley said, 'and he will. You see, Barney, I do keep my promises. All of them. That barn out back have a lock on it?' he asked Webb.

'A bar across the doors.'

'All right. Throw Clanahan in there. Latham? You and Quill take turns watching the barn — I wouldn't want him to have a chance of slipping away.'

I was escorted roughly across the dry

129

yard behind the house beneath star-filled skies. The hazy glow of the rising moon was just visible along the eastern horizon as a barn door was swung open and thick hands shoved me inside to land on my face in the horse-smelling interior. The door closed again, cutting off all light, and the bar fell heavily into its iron brackets. From some chink in the plank walls enough starlight leaked into the barn so that I caught its reflection in the bay horse's eye. I struggled to my feet, dusted off and went to the bay's stall, resting my hand on its neck. In the adjoining stall, I noticed now, stood Trish's roan pony. How then had she — ?

'What's this,' a soft voice inquired, 'the rescue party?' and Trish rose to her feet in the shadowed corner of the roan's stall.

'What are you doing here!' I asked in a hoarse whisper.

'Where else could I have gone without being seen?' she replied. 'I know Ned's horses, of course, and when I saw him riding this way surrounded by a group of men I did not know, I guessed there was trouble afoot. I didn't wait around to find out what it was. I made for the barn, hoping to retrieve my roan, but there wasn't enough time before they rode in — whoever they are.'

I told her, briefly, who they were and what had been happening.

'And now they're talking about massacring everyone on the Canoga?' she asked in disbelief.

'If Shockley gets his way.'

'No one could be that evil,' Trish said.

'Yes,' I answered miserably, 'someone could.' I was feeling defeated and futile. I turned from Trish and braced my hands against the stall, staring into the blackness. I felt Trish's hand touch my shoulder and slide down across my back before falling away.

I said, 'Maybe I just should have let well enough alone, like Shockley said. Let the counterfeit army run the settlers off their land.'

Trish said, 'Maybe you should have just ignored our problems altogether and run away, Giles.' There was a smile in her voice, a comforting tone that said she understood my frustration. 'All that being said, it's over and done with now. Where do we go from here?'

I looked back at the barred barn doors and asked, 'Where can we go? What is there left to try?'

'I don't know, but I'm not willing to give up. Are you, Giles?'

'No,' I said wearily, turning to look down at her, a shadowy, somehow reassuring presence standing near to me. 'Not yet.'

I fell silent then and Trish stood unmoving as if trying to penetrate my thoughts. 'What are you thinking?' she asked at length.

'I was wondering if maybe we ought just to let Cole come up the canyon trail. Maybe he could moderate Shockley's actions. There's something I don't understand about their relationship.'

'I don't suppose we'd be any worse off than we are now,' Trish said meditatively, 'but then we'd be greatly outnumbered in any fight.'

'I know it!' I said in a harsh whisper. The truth was I didn't see any way out of this. These men had come to bring war to the Canoga and would not be satisfied until it had been ignited.

'We have to get out of here first,' Trish said. 'I could try to warn all the remaining ranchers — to make sure they have their doors locked and rifles ready.'

'How do we get out, Trish?'

'We have one advantage,' she said. 'They still don't know that there are two of us in here.'

She was right. There would only be one man standing watch outside the barred door. If we could somehow lure him inside . . .

'Let's saddle the horses, Trish,' I said. That done, I approached the barn doors. I could hear someone nervously pacing outside, probably annoyed at having been posted out in the night, missing whatever discussion was taking place inside Trish's house. Which one was it? I wondered. Latham and Quill were the two names I had heard Shockley call. I supposed it didn't matter. I tried:

'Quill?' and got only silence in return. Louder I said, 'Quill?'

Quill growled a response. 'Shut up in there.'

'I have something to say to you.' Silence followed that as well. 'There's ten thousand in gold for you if you let me go.'

That too was followed by silence, but it seemed to be a thoughtful silence. Or maybe that was only wishful thinking. Long minutes passed before I heard the outlaw whisper mistrustfully.

'What the hell are you talking about?'

'I'm talking about ten thousand dollars in gold,' I said.

'Shut up. You haven't got ten bucks, likely.'

'Quill,' I said, my head leaning

against the barn door. 'Listen to me. You're in too deep with Shockley and his scheme. There's going to be a hell of a lot of fighting, men dying on both sides. And when Hammond Cole gets here, he's going to raise hell with Shockley as well. I know Cole,' I lied. 'He won't like this. Not after he worked out his plan so carefully.'

Again a long silence followed. Finally Quill asked, 'This gold you're talking about — where'd it come from?'

'From — ' I put exasperation into my voice. 'I can't keep talking to a door. Come in for a minute. No one else is around, is there?'

'Think I'm crazy!' Quill asked. 'You got anything to say, say it now.'

'I have something to say, yes. Ten thousand if you let me escape. My life is worth that to me. What can Jake do to you, cuss you out, slap you around? Listen, Quill, I can't talk through this damned door. I'll back off. Stand in the middle of the floor, my back to you.'

The silence this time was interminable.

I was beginning to think that my ploy had failed, that Quill's fear of Shockley was great enough to overcome his greed. I felt the barn doors push in, a bare inch. The bar was still in place in its iron brackets.

'Step over where I can see you, Clanahan,' he instructed me, 'and back to the middle of the barn. Turn your back. I'll give you two minutes to convince me.'

I backed to the center of the barn and then turned my back. I had only a fleeting glimpse of Trish standing beside one of the doors with the axe handle in her hands. The heavy oaken bar was lifted and placed aside. Quill slipped into the barn, glanced left and right, unable to see Trish behind the door, and took three steps toward me, his rifle aimed at my back.

'Tell me what the hell you're talking about, Clanahan. Talk straight and talk fast.'

I didn't have to do either. Before the last word had escaped Quill's lips, Trish had slipped from behind the door, raised the axe handle and slammed it down with all of her strength behind the outlaw's ear. He folded up without a sound and skidded on his face across the barn floor to lie motionless.

I snatched the rifle from Quill's inert hands and slipped his Colt from its holster, sliding it into my own. Trish stood there, trembling, axe handle still in her hand.

'Let's get moving,' I said urgently.

'Yes,' she nodded. Without a word between us we went to the stalls where our saddled horses stood and moved to the front of the barn. Outside it was silent; no one moved in the shadowed yard. Lights still blazed in Irish's window as I closed the barn doors, replaced the bar, and with Trish, led the horses from the clearing. Beyond the oaks we paused and swung into leather.

'Warn as many people as you can, Trish. Tell them to get everyone inside and lock down, ready for trouble.'

'You, Clanahan, what — ?'

'First I'm going back to the canyon. I made a mistake. Now I have to tell the Canoga ranchers what's happening back here. I'll send them home.'

'You'll be coming with them, won't you?' Trish asked. Her hair had mostly come free of its arrangement and now frizzed out in a moonlit halo once again. I had decided that I liked it that way better. Her eyes caught starlight and waited hopefully for my answer.

'No, Trish,' I said, when I could no longer remain silent. 'I won't be coming back with them. Find yourself a place to hole up in the strongest house you know of. Or . . . Trish, I wish you'd just ride away from all of this. There will be much fighting, much killing.'

'I've already told you that I won't run,' Trish said defiantly. Then, 'You're not going to tell me what you're going to do, are you?'

'No. You wouldn't like it and I don't want anyone to know.'

Frustration showed in her expression and in her voice, 'I don't think you

know what you're going to do at all!'
Then she swung her roan's head
around and heeled it into a rapid trot. I
watched her go, weaving through the
oaks, vanishing at last in the night
shadows. I hated parting that way. Not
knowing if I would ever even see her
again.

Glowering, I turned the bay horse
westward, retracing my tracks to the
head of the canyon where the Canoga
boys stood watch. I did know what I
was going to do, I just didn't know if it
made any sense at all. It was a
desperate plan that I had formulated
and I didn't want to tell Trish and have
her try to talk me out of it. I wanted to
do it and have done with it one way or
the other before I had the time to stop
and weigh the consequences. I rode on
through the night in the darkest mood
in memory.

'Hold up there,' a voice from the
darkness ordered as I reached the
trailhead.

'It's Clanahan,' I called out.

'Come ahead.'

I rode past the sentry — it was Dee Cobbold — and found the men gathered loosely together at the canyon rim, watching and waiting for Cole and his raiders. I swung down from my horse and walked up to them, their eyes studying me in the pale moonlight.

'What's happening, Clanahan?'

'Have there been any Cole men trying the trail?' I asked without answering.

'Three or four of them tried to sneak up the canyon about an hour ago,' Harold Kendrick told me. 'We scattered them with a few dozen rifle shots.'

'All right.' I looked around, squatting down in the middle of the knot of Canoga settlers. 'Can everybody hear me?'

'Charlie and Oliver Webb are sleeping. Want me to get them?' Gus Staley asked.

'No, let them have their rest. This doesn't concern them anyway. You've all got to return home.' Their faces wore puzzled disbelief. After all, I had practically begged them to ride out here and help me hold the canyon road against Cole and his men. But everything had changed. I hadn't been expecting an attack from the rear, nor could I have known Shockley's bloodthirsty plan of action. As quickly as possible, I told them what was happening back on the Canoga. Some of them were heading for their horses before I had even finished speaking.

'It might be a good idea for several families to fort up in one of the bigger houses,' I said. I got a collection of grunts, nods, indifferent shrugs in response.

'How 'bout you let us fight this battle our own way, Clanahan?' DeFord growled. 'You didn't do us a favor with your advice the first time — got us all out here leaving our homes and family unprotected.' He was one of those who had already swung into the saddle. 'If these raiders hit my spread while I'm out here . . . God help you if I cut your trail again.'

141

I couldn't blame him. DeFord was right. I had summoned them all away from their ranches, not knowing that Shockley was so close. What *had* brought Jake into the fight prematurely? According to Cole's plan he and his men were supposed to wait until the settlers had been forced from their land. And Jake could have had no way of knowing that Cole was bugged down in the canyon. I didn't like it. Not a bit.

Which was why I was going to do what I intended.

Sleepy-eyed, Charlie and Oliver Webb wandered toward me, Ollie with a blanket wrapped around his shoulders. They watched the Canoga men slap spurs to their horses and ride hard back toward the settlement. Frowning, Charlie asked:

'What's going on, Clanahan?'

I had to tell them. Tell them all — including the fact that their father had fallen in with the raiders, made a pact with them to improve his lot, that he and Wes King were traitors. I don't know how much of this they believed, how much they accepted. It's never easy to believe the worst of family. Oliver seemed dazed by the implications.

'What do we do, Charles?' he asked his older brother.

'What can we do?' Charlie answered with a sigh. 'We have to get back to the ranch.'

'That leaves Clanahan alone to watch the trail.'

'We'll just have to let them have it,' I said. 'It doesn't matter much anymore. Besides, it will take them a while to figure out that we've all pulled out.'

'All of us? You too, Clanahan? Where are you going?' Charlie asked. The friendliness that had always been in his eyes was gone now.

'I'm going down there,' I said, inclining my head toward Cole's distant troops.

'And do what!' Charlie exclaimed. Ollie was even more upset.

'He said he knew Cole, didn't he?

Maybe he's been working with the land grabbers all along, bringing all the ranchers over here while another group of raiders snuck in the back way.'

'It's not like that, Ollie,' I said evenly. 'I think you know that. I've been trying to help. I guess I'm just not very good at it. Now I think I can help by talking to Cole.'

'How? And how are you going to reach him? If you try the canyon they'll shoot you out of hand before you can make a hundred yards.'

'Yes, yes, they would,' I agreed. 'I mean to try riding the old Indian trail.'

'That's a fool idea,' Charlie said. 'It can't be done. At night!'

'I'm going to try. There's a moon.'

'Not much of one,' Ollie said, glancing eastward.

'I'm patient. I'll wait until it's riding high. Then I'm going to try riding the footpath. I've got to reach Cole, boys. I believe that's the only way to prevent a massacre.'

8

The trail I rode plunged deeper still into the dark bowels of hell. The pale moon was so dim as barely to cast a shadow of horse and man as we ever-so-cautiously picked our way down the mountainside. To my right the earth dropped off into the depths of oblivion, to the left a jutting wall of stone rose toward the stars. There was barely enough room for my horse to walk. My left stirrup brushed the stone bluff, my right dangled over the chasm below.

The Indian trail, nothing but an eroded footpath centuries old was littered with fallen stones and rutted by run-off from above. I was a fool to be riding it. I would have been foolish to walk it in daylight, but I saw no other way to accomplish what I hoped. Logically, it did not matter if I plunged to my death, since behind lay Jake

Shockley and his noose and ahead Hammond Cole's army, but logic could do nothing to settle the nerve-breaking fear of falling to my death in the unknown, unseen reaches of the abyss.

The bay balked continually, but I could not allow it to halt. To back or turn around was impossible, and so I urged the old army horse forward gently but firmly, hoping its instincts were sharp enough to keep its skittering hoofs on the broken trail. We inched our way downward for a hundred bone-chilling minutes.

Then the bay halted, and I could not urge it forward. Bending forward, I saw the reason for its refusal. The trail ahead had washed out deeply. A swale had been cut across it ten feet deep and perhaps thirty feet across. The bay balked and could not be urged to attempt crossing the rubble cluttered wash.

I had to dismount. There was no other way. Easing my left leg across the bay's neck I clung to the saddlehorn and slid cautiously to the ground. Only my boot toes found purchase. The grip I had on my pommel was all that was keeping me from plummeting downward. Tediously, cautiously, I inched my boots forward, sliding them along the very rim of the trail. Small rocks came loose beneath my feet and slid away down the cliffside. I eased around the bay's shoulder, holding on to its bridle for balance, praying that it would not shy. I managed to get both boots planted firmly on level ground as I slipped past the horse's nose. Still I could raise my arm and touch the face of the cliff. That was how narrow the trail was. I did not pause to think about matters. I took a deep breath and let myself slip into the wash, still holding the bay's reins.

The bottom of the washout was filled with hundreds of small red rocks. I shifted my feet carefully so as not to disturb them, and turned, looking up at the broken edge of trail on the far side of the depression. It looked to be ten feet up, slightly higher than I could reach. There was no choice. I brought the bay down into the depression where it stood quivering beside me.

It was a dangerous thing to do, but I looped the end of the horse's reins around my belt at the back and searched for purchase. My hand found a dry, protruding root and I tugged on it, testing its strength. It seemed able to bear my weight, so with a sigh, I planted my boot on a boulder, pulled myself up and slid over on to the trail above. I lay there for a minute, my heart pounding. The tug of the bay on the reins stirred me to action. If it balked . . .

I untied the reins from my belt and stood facing the horse. I murmured, pled, commanded the bay to follow me up. If I could not urge it out of the wash it would stand there until it fell, and lie until it was hide and bones. With equine resignation the old war horse started forward. Rocks rolled free and it tossed its head desperately, but eventually, following orders, it managed to scramble awkwardly up on to the flats to stand quivering. I stroked the beast and tried to quiet it with my words. We were not yet halfway down the mountainside and I needed the animal to be calm and trusting.

The trail was just wide enough for me to mount normally — though from the wrong side — and we continued down the broken trail.

An hour along the path widened into something like a road and we began to pass through twisted cedar trees and stunted piñon pines, the trail gradually flattening until sometime after midnight the vista opened and I found myself looking out across the long desert.

I let the horse breathe, relax its tormented muscles, and I scanned the limitless flats before me. Eventually we started on again. The more dangerous part of the night still lay ahead. We had descended into hell and now it was time to meet the devil.

The moon was coasting toward the western horizon, leaving a glitter of stars in its wake when I saw the white canvas of the covered wagons plain against the black background. Nearing the camp I saw a remuda of horses, two men far distant, standing watch at the mouth of the canyon trail. My jaw was clamped so tightly that my teeth ached as I neared, expecting a bullet at any time although they didn't figure to be trigger happy in the near-darkness, firing at an unidentified target.

I knew which was Cole's wagon. I had noticed while I was among them that his was the only one with 'US' stenciled large on its canvas. Picking it out, I swung down and led my horse through the quiet camp, smelling the dead wood fires, the vaguest trace of bacon long cooked and consumed. It was enough to make my stomach remind me that my last meal lay in the almost unremembered past.

I had taken a dozen steps into the perimeter of the silent camp when the voice behind me issued a challenge.

'Who goes there? Stand where you are and hoist your hands high.'

I thought I recognized the voice, and as I stood like a scarecrow waiting for the shadowy figure to brace me, I discovered that I was right.

'Hello, Sergeant Hawkins.'

'Oh, it's you, is it?' the big man replied not unpleasantly. 'You won't be needing this wherever you're going,' he said, relieving me of my Colt. 'You came back on your own? I always figured you were a little crazy.'

'I guess I am.' I had to agree. He had eased around so that he stood facing me, his own pistol leveled at my belt buckle.

'You can lower your hands.' He tipped his cap back and grimaced with pained amusement. 'What in blazes are you doing back here, Clanahan?'

'I want to see Cole.'

'Oh, you will! Don't doubt that.' At

151

his gesture I started walking toward the bandit leader's wagon.

'Also I brought Kirk's horse back.'

'I'm sure he'll appreciate that,' the broad shouldered sergeant said, 'he's been doing a lot of walking lately. By the way, how are your feet?'

'Much better, thanks.'

'Glad to hear it.' I couldn't measure Hawkins's attitude. He seemed sincere, but probably he was only having fun with the poor imbecile who, once free, would voluntarily ride back into the outlaw camp.

Nearing Cole's wagon I could now see a lantern burning so low that I hadn't noticed it before, and silhouetted by its faint glow was a woman sitting on the tailgate, her long dark hair loose around her shoulders. She glanced up, frowned and then flashed a surprised smile.

'Well, well. You decided to rejoin us.' Beth Cole turned her head and called into the wagon. 'Hammond — we have a visitor!' As Hawkins's voice had sounded pleasant, so did Beth Cole's sound cheerful as if we were all old friends come together once more. When Hammond Cole appeared from behind the canvas flaps of the covered wagon, his expression wore no mask.

'I'll be damned! Where'd you find this idiot, Hawkins?'

'Just walked up to me, sir. Says he wanted to talk to you.'

'I want to talk to him as well,' Cole said, swinging lithely down from the tailgate. His movements were panther-like, and I could easily see the anger in his eyes, the clenched muscles of his jaw.

'Cole, I need to speak to you.'

'Shut up!' he exploded.

'It's about Jake Shockley,' I told him, and his expression altered instantly. His eyes became thoughtful, then angry again, then assumed an interrogator's blank curiosity.

'What about him?' he asked carefully.

'He's jumped the gun. He's already on the Canoga and ready to make his move. He's not waiting for you.'

Cole smothered a curse, glanced at Beth who shook her head, then told Hawkins, 'I won't need you, Sergeant. Let me have Clanahan's pistol.' We waited in silence for a minute as Hawkins strode away, then Cole hissed at me: 'What do you know of Shockley, and how — ?'

'I know just about everything about him, the plan to take the Canoga, about the double-cross,' I said, seeing Cole flinch at the last word.

'Then it *was* Jake who started the landslide that blocked the canyon,' Cole said. I did not correct this mistaken assumption. 'You said you know all about matters, how is that?' he demanded of me.

'Simple. Jake took me prisoner — you know he was looking for me. While I was being held he talked to a few of the ranchers. I overheard it all. He figures to go ahead without you. Not using guile, but simply slaughtering all of the settlers on the land. He's going to try blaming it on the Indians.'

'No one could be that stupid!' Cole said. His smoldering eyes met Beth's. Her mouth tightened.

'It's true,' the woman said. 'It has to be. Why would Clanahan show up here with such a wild tale?'

'Why are you here, Clanahan?' Cole demanded.

'I want you to restore order, Cole. Jake Shockley is a mad dog. He's bent on slaughter as a means to an end. I might not approve of what you had in mind, but it was theft not murder you intended. You know, Cole, you'll be held accountable for whatever Jake does now. He's spread your name around. It's no secret that you were the mastermind behind this. If one man talks, you'll hang for Shockley's crimes.' I looked at Beth, trying to gauge the look in those dark eyes. 'Everyone involved will be headed for the gallows.'

'How could he hope to get away with it?' Cole asked. 'He can't believe the army, all of the civilian authorities, are

stupid enough to accept his preposter-
ous story at face value. They *know* all
about Jake Shockley's criminal career.
And tell me, Clanahan, have you ever
heard of an Indian uprising on a scale
such as the one Jake means to stage, in
which not a single man, woman or child
survived? And that's what he would
have to do, isn't it? That's what you are
implying that he will do.'

'I'm not implying it. I'm telling you
straight out that I heard Jake give that
order to his men.'

Cole closed his eyes then looked
again at Beth. Their eyes met deeply,
exchanging thoughts I could only guess
at. Cole said: 'I'm ruined. All of the
months of planning. Getting the men
together. The uniforms and army
horses. The forged documents. Ruined!
Damn him to hell!'

Beth said, 'I could have told you,
Hammond. Father can always be
trusted to take advantage of anyone.'

'Father?' I said aloud, without meaning to.

'Yes,' Beth said as if none of their secrets mattered any more. 'Jake Shockley, the bloody bastard, is my father.'

Which explained how the two groups had fallen in together, but —

'Then, Cole, is Shockley your — ?' I began.

'No, damnit, he's not *my* father. I know you're not bright, Clanahan, but you couldn't really believe that Beth is my sister. We share the Cole name because she's my wife.'

I *had* known, really, or at least suspected it. I didn't care for Cole's characterization of me, but perhaps he was right. Look at where my brilliance had landed me.

'What do you think, Beth?' Cole was asking. Her answer was long in coming and spoken carefully.

'I think you have to try to stop him, Hammond. Clanahan is right, you know. You will hang if Jake does what he has in mind . . . all of us. There won't be a safe place to hide in in all the Territory.'

'We can't go all the way around again,' Cole said, considering matters. 'There isn't time. With the canyon trail blocked, with sharpshooters above — '

'There's no one left up there,' I told the outlaw leader. 'I just passed that a few hours ago.'

'You're sure?' he asked suspiciously. 'Because if you're lying — '

'I'm sure. It would be a slow ride, but your soldiers can pick their way up the road, even by moonlight. Maybe,' I said optimistically, 'you can talk Jake out of this crazy idea of his. You've got three times the men he does and — '

'No one talks Jake Shockley out of anything,' his daughter put in, 'unless he has him at gunpoint. Even then it's not a certain prospect. Don't ask me how I know. I just do. I lived with the man for almost twenty years.'

'No, you're right,' Cole agreed. 'It will become a gun battle, no two ways about it. And we'll have the ranchers against us as well.'

'Maybe not,' I told Cole. 'They know

that the army has been summoned from Camp Grant — or at least they think that's the case. They have no way of knowing that you aren't the regular army. Only a couple of turncoat ranchers know the true facts.'

'And you know where Shockley is? Right now?'

'Yes,' I said.

'You'll lead us to him?'

'Yes.'

'We have to try it, Cole,' Beth said, and I saw Hammond Cole smile with bitterness.

'Fighting for another lost cause,' the ex-Confederate said dryly. 'Yes, darling girl, I suppose we must.'

I asked a question that had been nagging me: 'Who killed Brad Champion?'

'Who?' Cole asked blankly.

'Champion, You know, the kid on reconnaissance,' Beth provided.

'Him?' Cole said. 'How would I know? The boys with him said that he he had fallen for some girl up on the

Canoga. We figured he deserted to be with her.'

It had to have been Barney Webb who had done it then. Alone or with the aid of Wes King. The Webb boys had told me that they had been friends with Champion, that they had spent much time in his company. Barney Webb could have seen that as a threat to the plans he had made with Jake Shockley. He might have gunned young Brad Champion down fearing that his three sons would learn too much from the former Cole rider.

'Brad Champion,' Cole was saying. 'Why do you ask about him, Clanahan? Is he the one that triggered off all this trouble?'

'No, Cole, he isn't. It was you who started this all in motion, you and your greed. Now, maybe, you have the chance to make amends. Now are you going to slink away and hide, washing your hands of the affair, or do we ride to the Canoga?'

9

The Canoga lay spread out before us bathed in the soft glow of the descending three-quarter moon. The dew clinging to the long grass gleamed faintly and the scattered ponds were splashed with silver. The leaves of the oak trees growing in small clumps among the tilled fields were moon-glossed; smoke rose in lazy curlicues from the chimneys of the scattered houses. The Canoga resembled more a fairyland setting than the bloody battlefield it would become.

The ride up the canyon had been demanding in the near-darkness, our horses picking their way among the tumbled rocks. I rode the bay horse once again; there was no mention of returning it to Kirk. The affable Sergeant Hawkins rode beside me the entire way. I could not tell if it was his choice to do so or if he had been assigned to guard me. I knew that no one had returned my guns.

Reaching the flats, resting our horses briefly, Hawkins and I had fallen into a conversation. It seemed important to him to justify Cole's actions to me, and I listened without much comment.

'Have you been watching Captain Hammond?' the big man asked, wiping his brow with a bandanna. 'All he needs is a saber in his hand and it would be like old times. All of the men riding with us are from his old battalion, you know. Men who lost everything and had no place to settle and start over after the war. The captain felt like he owed them something for their service. He wanted to pay them back for their years of fighting under him.'

'An admirable feeling,' I commented, 'but it seems to me that he chose the wrong way to show his gratitude.'

'You'd never understand how it was,' Hawkins said heavily. 'The Union army destroyed everything they could and then the flood of carpetbaggers stole what little remained.'

'You're right, Hawkins, I'll never understand that part of it. But I know that stealing the homes and property of other people, innocent people, is wrong no matter the justification.'

Hawkins looked at me and smiled gently, a faraway expression. 'Ah,' he said meaninglessly, 'you are so young. But then! You've won, Clanahan, so it makes no difference, does it? Somehow this has turned into a grand adventure — a chance for the captain, all of us, to fight for a just cause once again.'

I followed Hawkins's words well enough, but his conclusions escaped me. As for me having won anything . . . what, exactly had I won? I had begun a bloody conflict that probably would not have occurred had it not been for my meddling. Nonetheless, the die had been cast, and there was nothing to do but proceed.

'I'll need my guns sooner or later,' I said.

'Sooner or later the captain will have them returned,' Hawkins said expressionlessly. The lead riders had started forward and so we heeled our horses on, riding in double file deeper into the settlement.

We were close enough to the front that I could see Cole's straight back as he led us onward, feel the pride he felt. Riding beside him was the one person I did admire but did not understand. Beth Cole. What was she thinking? Was she torn between loyalty to her husband and devotion to her father? She had certainly shown no liking for Jake Shockley, but that could have been façade. She nevertheless rode on bravely beside her husband, apparently having no fear of battle or death. I wished now that I had had more time to talk to Beth, to know her. It had been impossible at the time of course, and now would never happen.

Besides, I reminded myself, neither of us might even live out this night.

It began before any of us was

prepared for it. We were filing past a field of alfalfa nearly ready for the mowing. A dozen oak trees stood in a clump near the trail. From the dark shadows of the trees gunshots suddenly erupted. Flame flashed from the muzzles of rifles; a man in front of me clutched at his chest and fell from his horse. The rest of the soldiers scattered. Sergeant Hawkins grabbed the bridle to my bay and shouted above the racketing of the rifles, 'This way!'

Ahead of us a drainage ditch ran paralleling the field. Hawkins intended that we should take cover there. I ducked low across the withers and heeled my horse that way as other soldiers rushed past us, firing as they rode. I dismounted on the run and sprawled to earth in the muddy ditch. Hawkins never reached it.

A bullet fired from the oak grove struck him in the throat. Blood fountained from the wound. I saw instantly that it was a killing shot and could only watch helplessly as Hawkins fought to stay in the saddle, to achieve the shelter of the drainage ditch, and fell dead in the roadway, the following riders leaping their horses over his body.

Captain Cole had regrouped his men a little way ahead and now, with a few hand signals, dispatched his soldiers. These formed two flanking groups and, surrounding the oak grove, they opened fire from horseback. Then, half a dozen men who had been concealed in the trees, broke free of the encirclement, whipping their horses toward safety, the soldiers pursuing them.

I waited. The descending moon lit Hawkins's empty eyes. There was not another man to be seen across the fields in any direction. I clawed my way up out of the ditch and walked to Hawkins, leading my bay horse. I slipped his Colt revolver from his holster, collected his Winchester rifle and shoved it into my saddle scabbard. For Hawkins I could do nothing but bid him a silent farewell.

I found his horse, reins trailing, fifty

yards on. Distant gunfire crackled, but I saw no living soul. I gathered up the reins to Hawkins's horse, figuring I might need it.

Trish might need it — if I could only find her.

That was my plan now: to find her and take her far away from the Canoga. No matter what happened between the warring factions. To rescue her and ride far away from here even if I had to take her kicking and screaming to safety. I wanted her well, and I had had enough of all this trouble.

I did not know where she had gone. I had told her to try to hole up in one of the stronger ranch houses, but I did not know if she had followed my instructions. Nor did I know which house she might have taken shelter in or even where any of the ranches were located.

And I did not know if I could convince her to ride with me.

Her loyalty to her dead father, to the ranch they had built together, to her neighbors, was obvious. She loved the

Canoga country and was willing to fight for it. What influence could I wield that would overcome those feelings? The answer was discouraging. None. None at all. I rode on with only groundless hope to sustain me.

I saw the lone rider approaching before he saw me and I was able to guide my horses into the shadows of a lone, wide-spreading oak tree. I waited, rifle at the ready. The moon was lowering and on this increasingly dark night it was difficult to tell friend from foe — assuming I had any friends left on the Canoga. As he neared, I recognized the rider and called out to him.

'Oliver!'

Looking startled, Ollie Webb reined up the piebald pony he was riding and squinted into the shadows, his rifle at the ready. I rode on to the road to meet him.

'Oh,' he said, with undisguised contempt, 'it's you.'

'How's everything in the settlement?' I asked.

'Mostly quiet.' His words were bitten off sharply. He studied me with angry eyes. 'You did it, Clanahan, didn't you?'

'Did it?'

'As soon as you got the rest of us out of the canyon, you rode down and led the raiders up here.'

'I did,' I was forced to admit. 'But you have to understand my thinking.'

'I don't,' he said sharply before I could go further with my explanation. 'It seems my father was right about you all along. He was alerted as soon as we rode back to the ranch and told him what had happened. He gathered a few men and rode out to try to head the land grabbers off.'

So it was Webb and his crowd who had ambushed Cole's army and not, as I had believed, Jake Shockley's men.

'Where are you riding now, Oliver?' I asked.

'To try catching up with my father. They're greatly outnumbered.'

'Where's Charlie?'

'My brother still doesn't see the truth

of what you've done. For some reason he still trusts you. As if you could trust someone who has let the enemy in your back door. What did they promise you, Clanahan? Money? Land?'

'Nobody promised me anything,' I said coldly. I was sorry that Oliver saw things the way he did, but I understood. In his place maybe I would have felt the same way. 'Where's Trish?' I asked. 'Have you seen her?'

'At the Staley place,' Oliver told me. 'She was there trying to talk to some of the men when we got word that you had let the outlaw army ride the canyon trail.'

'Some day, Ollie, when there's time, I'll explain it all to you.'

His eyes told me that he had no desire to hear anything more from me. I still was not sure that he wouldn't start shooting. I don't think he had decided either. Risking it, I nodded, and started the horses forward, showing him my back.

I wasn't sure where the Staley ranch

was, but I knew the direction the others had taken when riding to the spread from Trish's house. I thought I could find the place even in the darkness.

After that? Well, I just didn't know. What I wanted and what Trish was determined to do were at wide variance. My idea was to ride away, see that she was safe and then maybe, when things played out, to return to the Canoga with her. She intended to stay and fight for her land, I knew. I did not want to present myself to her as a coward; neither did I wish to die fighting a battle that seemed desperately doomed. The only hope was of Cole defeating Jake Shockley's outlaw band and giving up the land grab as a bad bargain now that he and his men had been exposed as counterfeit soldiers.

It seemed a vague hope. I did not doubt that Cole could defeat Jake, but what of his own men? They had been promised land and homes, would they all be willing to put down their arms and simply ride away with nothing to show for their efforts?

These thoughts drifted through my mind as I rode the dark trail toward the Staley ranch. Full darkness was settling as the moon died in the west and the night seemed much colder, more dangerous still.

I saw the white two-story house beyond the surrounding trees, its lights blazing, and I started that way. I nearly bumped into the armed man emerging from the shadows.

'Charlie!' I said with relief. He smiled weakly at me and eased his pony up beside mine. 'If you're looking for Oliver, he's about three miles down the road.'

'I'm not,' Charlie said quietly, nervously. 'I'm standing picket. Lucky I recognized you. I was about to sound the alarm.'

'How many men do you have in the house?' I asked and I thought that Charlie paused uncertainly before answering. Perhaps he was still not sure of me

172

and thought I had devious reasons for asking.

At last he told me, 'A dozen or so.'

'And Trish?' I asked, trying to keep my anxiousness from showing. Charlie Webb shook his head.

'She's gone, Clanahan.'

'Gone!' I said in disbelief. She had found a relatively safe place to ride out the storm and then had decided to ride off. Why?

'She wasn't comfortable here. Said she wanted to be back at her place. Said she could fight as well there as from here, better maybe.'

'She's crazy!' I said in disbelief. Charlie grinned.

'She does seem to tilt that way,' he agreed, adding: 'She was figuring — after hearing the shooting on the western trail, that the battle had begun and that Shockley — is that his name? — must have abandoned her house and gone on the attack.'

'It wasn't Jake Shockley who was doing the shooting.' I told him, 'it was your father and whoever's riding with him.'

'Oh,' Charlie said, pursing his lips. 'Yeah, that figures, doesn't it?'

It did because Barney Webb would do anything to curry favor with Jake Shockley. The return of his sons from the canyon must have given him warning that Cole might have attempted the ride up to the Canoga.

'Is she alone, Charlie?' I asked.

'Ned went with her,' he replied.

'Ned!'

'Yeah, he's a little puppy dog where Trish is concerned. He wouldn't let her go alone. No one else offered.'

'I've got to get over there,' I said. My despair must have been obvious. I couldn't help it. Trish, alone except for a kid barely out of short trousers, riding into Jake Shockley's camp!

'I'd go with you, Clanahan,' Charlie said, 'but you see how it is.'

'I know. Thanks for wanting to help. The army was pursuing your father and his crowd to the south. If anyone wishes to attack the house, they'll likely not be riding up the western road.'

'Thanks, Clanahan. And good luck to you.'

Luck. I needed a lot of luck, and it seemed I must have already used up my fair share in the last few days. What had impelled Trish to ride back to her house, knowing that it was an outlaw fortress? I knew, of course. How many times had she told me that she was going to fight for her land? She meant it and I could only admire her for the vow she had made, but her concept of how to go about things was seriously flawed.

I rode on through the darkness, wondering if my own thinking was not just as flawed. A lone knight rushing to the rescue of a maiden who seemed not to want rescuing.

I rode southward, still hearing occasional gunfire crackling toward the east as the forces of evil fought the forces of evil. Viewed in that light there seemed to be a sort of madness to it. Jake Shockley could not win, outnumbered as he was, Cole could not win now that his plan had fallen apart. Barney Webb had already lost. The day he had thrown in with Jake had been the end of him. Once the community learned of his and Wes King's treachery, they would no longer be welcome neighbors on the Canoga.

The moon was only a memory beyond the eastern hills, but by starlight I pressed the bay horse on toward Trish's tiny house, wondering what rash course she might have followed. I guessed that she had believed her house by now would be empty of raiders, they having gone to join the battle. On her own, and now with the help of young Ned Webb, she would drop the shutters and bar the door, ready and willing to hold off any interlopers with her Winchester.

Perhaps she was right. I saw no reason why Shockley would take the time and trouble to assault her. He had much bigger problems to deal with. Still, you never knew what some men might do. Especially a man obsessed like Jake Shockley.

Maybe his gang, seeing that the game was up, had decided to pull out while they could. More unlikely, but chillingly possible — maybe Jake and Cole had managed to reach a truce and had formulated a new course of action. Maybe anything!

I only knew that I had to find Trish and be at her side when trouble did come. I felt that way about her now; I had felt that way since I found her alone and wandering in the desert. It was a fine feeling, caring for her that way, but I couldn't convince myself that she felt the same about me, no matter that I was a 'fine looking specimen'.

I could smell woodsmoke long before I spotted the little house concealed among the oaks. I swung down from my horse and led it forward through the star-shadows, rifle in my hand. Approaching from the rear, I could not see how many horses might be hitched in the front of the house, and circling that way, putting myself in the line of fire, seemed ill-advised. I dropped the reins to the bay horse and eased forward, finally sliding along the unpainted wall of the ranch house to the rear window. Cautiously I lifted my head and peered in.

Whatever I had expected to see, the group gathered within was not it.

In one corner sat Jake Shockley. Vallejo was beside him, seated on the floor. Across the room, sitting on the yellow sofa was Beth Cole! Facing them all, pistol in her hand, was Trish.

10

I slipped around the corner of the house, moving quickly — and silently, I hoped — toward the front door. I saw no men posted outside and there was no sign of Ned Webb. Just four horses, all of which I recognized.

How in the world had Trish gotten the drop on the badmen, and where had Beth Cole come from? What would she be doing here alone unless Cole had been cut down in the gun battle? I made my way to the plank door and knocked cautiously, keeping my body to one side of the door frame. I heard Trish's voice.

'Who is it?' She did not sound anxious.

'Giles. Let me in.'

'Who is it?' someone else — Vallejo, I thought — muttered.

'Clanahan.'

The response to this was a disparaging grunt. The door opened a bare inch and then was swung wide — by Beth Cole, smiling brightly as if I were a welcome sight. Trish stood leaning against the wall, one hand still holding the big Colt revolver, the other tucked under her arm. Her eyes flickered toward me.

'Took you long enough,' she said.

'No one invited me.' I glanced around at Shockley and the slumped Vallejo. Their faces showed only resignation. 'Where's Ned?' I asked Trish.

'Gone to try again,' she said. 'Maybe he will reach Camp Grant this time.'

'You still think we will need soldiers?' I asked. She answered tightly:

'*I'm* not going to hang all these thugs and killers.'

'No, I guess not,' I said, easing past Beth toward Trish. 'How did this happen?' I gestured toward the two prisoners. 'And Beth . . . how do you happen to be here?'

'This was easy,' Trish told me. Her

dark blue eyes were sparkling as she spoke. 'The three raiders must have decided to pull out. One of them was seeing to the horses while these two ransacked the house.' Looking around I could see that cupboards had been gone through, that the mattress on the bed in the other room had been flung aside.

'You said there were three men,' I commented.

'There were. The other one's in the barn. Ned got him.'

'It appears that I missed all of the action.' I said. There seemed to be a hint of derision in Trish's smile.

'So it seems.'

'And Beth?' I turned to her questioningly.

'Oh, Clanahan,' she said with weary exasperation. 'I found out where my father was from one of the men we captured. I had the idea that I could ride over here and talk to him before both he and Cole managed to get themselves killed.'

Her eyes grew misty. 'All I accomplished was distracting Father while this woman and her little man slipped in and got the drop on them.'

Jake Shockley, uncharacteristically, had said nothing to this point. Now he mumbled, 'Damn sloppy of me, wasn't it?'

Sloppy, yes. But fortuitous. If Jake hadn't had his attention diverted by the unexpected arrival of his daughter, things might have turned out much worse for Trish and Ned.

Jake said, 'Looks like instead of me hanging you, you've got the chance to kill me again, doesn't it, Clanahan?' Neither woman knew what Shockley meant, but it brought a thin smile to Vallejo's lips.

'I wouldn't think of doing that, Jake. I mean to take you back with me to Mesa Grande. There's still the small matter of that murder that I'd like to clear up.'

'That!' Jake Shockley said in surprise. 'They've already forgotten about that.

There's no way anyone is going to keep trying to track you down for that killing.'

'I'm not willing to take that risk,' I answered.

Vallejo had been stretching his arms and legs. I turned my eyes on him, wondering what he was up to. But I had been watching the wrong man. Jake Shockley suddenly reached for his boot and came up with a small, chrome-plated pistol. He fired before I could move, and he had taken the obvious shot — at the person holding the gun on him. In horror I saw his bullet tag Trish, saw crimson blood stain the sleeve and bodice of her white blouse. I was on Jake before he could fire again. Wrenching the pistol from his hand I slugged him as hard as I could on the jaw and he sagged back. Vallejo had been too surprised to make a move. Now I backed away from the prisoners, hearing Trish moaning softly on the floor behind me. I tossed the pistol to Beth.

'Keep an eye on them,' I told her, and I went to Trish. Lifting her head, I propped it with a cushion from the couch and then cut away the sleeve on her dress. The bullet had tagged her just below the shoulder joint, a difficult place to apply a tourniquet, but I did the best I could, using the strip of sleeve I had cut off. Dark blue eyes opened to look at me, to study me as I bound her wound. She smiled distantly and mouthed three words.

I had done all I could for the moment, and so I stroked her frizzy blond hair and stood to take care of the business at hand. First I meant to bind Shockley and Vallejo tightly so there would be no repetition or attempt at escape. With that in mind I went into the ravaged kitchen searching for twine or whatever I could find.

Returning, I found Shockley sitting up, rubbing his jaw. I felt like hitting him again. Glancing at Trish, bloody and unconscious, I felt like pummeling him half to death. Tying him up would have to do for now. I started that way but was halted mid-stride.

'That's far enough, Clanahan,' Beth Cole said calmly. 'You've done enough damage.' She had the little chrome pistol trained on me, and there was not a glimmer of a smile on her full lips. 'All right, Father, take his gun,' she said and, grinning wildly, Jake Shockley rose and stepped to me, yanking my Colt from its holster.

'I think I will hang you after all, Clanahan. You're just a — '

At that moment the front door banged open and Ned Webb appeared. He crouched and fired as Jake swung his pistol's muzzle toward the kid. Shockley got off the first shot, but his bullet flew wild, singing off into the night distances. Ned's shot was true. It took Jake high on the chest, stopping his heart and the bad man slumped to the floor, blood gurgling from his mouth.

Beth screamed and belatedly decided to fire her weapon at Ned, but I was near enough to grab her wrist and the barrel of her gun, twisting it out of her grasp. Ned's eyes were wide and he was trembling a little. Now I saw his eyes shift and the muzzle of his gun lift again. Behind me I heard the scuttling as Vallejo launched himself up off the floor toward me.

'Not him!' I shouted at a confused Ned Webb. Vallejo collided with me, fists swinging wildly. I threw a short hard left into his wind and then smashed my forearm into his face, and he staggered back, hit the wall and slid to the floor, blood streaming from his broken nose.

Ned had stepped behind me and knelt now beside Trish, concern obvious in his eyes.

'I'm glad I killed him,' he murmured to me. 'Shooting a woman . . . shooting Trish!'

'Where did you come from, Ned? I thought you were on your way to the fort.'

'Blasted horse stepped in a squirrel

hole, broke its leg.' He looked again at Trish and added sadly. 'I'm glad it did. Horse wasn't no good anyway.'

I returned my attention to Beth Cole, but the heart seemed to have gone out of her. She sat on the sofa, hands clasped between her knees, staring at her dead father. I wondered —

'Why did you really come here, Beth?'

'To warn Father, to let him know that Cole was after him.'

'But why?'

'Because he was my father, damnit! Is that so hard to understand?'

No, I supposed it wasn't.

Ned Webb paid no attention as I tied up Beth — loosely, but well enough to prevent further shenanigans. He was too busy keeping a mournful watch over Trish. I went to him and suggested, 'Let's put her in on her bed, shall we?'

Beth, seated on the yellow sofa, her head lolling back on her fine ivory neck stared at the ceiling, uninterested in anything about her. Jake lay dead;

Vallejo had managed to sit up groggily, his hands now tied behind him.

'Why did you keep me from plugging him?' Ned asked, as we re-entered the living room, leaving Trish, unconscious but with a strong pulse, on her bed. He indicated the battered Vallejo who lifted his miserable eyes to us.

'He,' I told Ned, 'is the only witness to the killing back in Mesa Grande. You'd know nothing about it, but Jake Shockley shot a man and blamed it on me. I need Vallejo alive. He and I are going to be taking a little ride together when matters are settled here.'

Ned nodded and then lifted his head alertly, 'There's a rider coming in,' he said. Listening, I could hear the sound of a single horse being ridden hard, approaching the house.

'Stay ready,' I said, and Ned took up a position at a loop in one of the front window shutters. Beth's eyes were excited now, perhaps hoping for rescue. I dashed cold water on her hopes.

'You'd better hope it's not Cole,' I

told her. 'I have a word or two to say to him.'

'He won't believe you,' she hissed.

'Won't he? How else are you going to explain your being here, Beth? He'll know that you turned traitor on him.'

'He won't — ' But she was interrupted by Ned's shout.

'It's Ollie!'

After peering out to make sure no one was following, I swung the front door open to admit Ned's trail-dusty brother. He stamped in, looked around in puzzlement and told us, 'Father's dead. It's all over for us.'

'What happened?' Ned asked, his excitement brimming over.

'Let me sit down,' Ollie said wearily, 'and I'll tell you.'

Dragging a wooden chair from the kitchen, I offered it to Oliver Webb who sat down heavily, briefly buried his face in his hands and told us, 'Father, Wes King and their riders ambushed Cole on the western road. Then, outnumbered, they had to flee across country.

Cole's men rode them down. The fighting was intense — could hear it from a distance — but short-lived. When I reached the battle site, I found Father just clinging to life. I sat him up and he said, 'I got him. Tell Jake Shockley that I killed Cole.''

Beth released a muffled, desperate cry. Oliver glanced that way and then continued.

'It was true, I found Cole's body not a quarter of a mile on. I found Wes King as well, also dead.'

'What happened to Cole's army, Oliver?' I asked.

'I don't know. Either they're regrouping somewhere or they just gave it up, what with Cole not there to urge them on. I don't think any of them wanted to fight much.'

'Maybe not,' I said. 'They didn't sign up for a fight. It wasn't supposed to work that way. And I imagine they had all seen enough of war to last them a lifetime.'

'Maybe,' Oliver agreed. 'But we'll be ready for them if they have second thoughts and decide to come back.' He nodded at the dead man, 'That's Shockley, isn't it? Where is the rest of his gang?'

'I don't know. Vallejo?'

The battered outlaw raised his head. 'Rode off,' he muttered through swollen lips. 'Latham, Quill — all of them. When this . . . person,' he said savagely, staring at Beth Cole, 'came in and told Jake that we would have to face an army if we wanted the land. There wasn't nobody that wanted a patch of dirt that bad.'

'Except you.'

'I rode with Jake, not for land. It was always me, Jake and Curt.'

'Where's Curt?'

'He was the first one out the door,' Vallejo said with savage bitterness. Then he closed his eyes and fell silent.

Trish's moan from the other room caught our attention. 'Anyone feel like risking a ride?' I asked. 'Trish needs better nursing than I can offer.'

'I'll go,' Ned volunteered. 'My

mother used to work for a doctor. She knows a lot about medicine.'

His brother stopped him on his way to the door, 'No need to say anything about Father yet,' Ollie cautioned him. Ned nodded his understanding and went out. The door was barred behind him. We still had no way of knowing who might be prowling the night.

Leaving Oliver to watch Beth and Vallejo, I went to Trish's bedside. I sat next to her, holding her hand. She was pale, very pale and her blouse was stained to deep crimson. She would be all right, I told myself.

She had to be.

I didn't glance at the clock, but hours passed and the stars swam slowly past beyond the cabin confines. It was in the early morning that I felt Trish stir, and when I looked at her, I saw the sparkle in those deep blue eyes.

'Giles,' was all she said, and that with effort, but she squeezed my hand and smiled before falling back into a deep sleep, and it was enough to satisfy me.

Epilogue

By the time I got back from Mesa Grande, taking the long way around to skirt the sand dunes, Trish was on her feet and busy. Her right arm was still in a sling, but she thought that another week would eliminate the need for that contraption. The army from Fort Grant had arrived in my absence. Trish told me about it as we sat on her front porch, watching the soft orange glow of sunset above the distant hills.

The army had rounded up a few of Cole's men who had lingered on the Canoga and also captured Curt who they had more than a passing interest in. It seems that he and several other Shockley gang members had attempted to waylay an army payroll a few months back.

'Beth Cole will go free,' Trish guessed. 'They really have no crime to charge her with. She will make out; women like her always find a way to survive.'

Trish went on to say that Beth had been flirting shamelessly with the lieutenant commanding the army force and that he hadn't been shy in his attentions to her either. 'If it is up to him, they'll probably pin a medal on her!' Trish laughed. I liked her laugh — merry, deep-throated. I hadn't really heard it until recently. It made a charming counter-point to the singing of the night birds as they gathered in the oaks.

'What about you?' Trish asked. 'You're here. They must have listened to Vallejo.'

'Yes, yes, they did,' I replied, and went on to tell her about the hearing in Mesa Grande which had required me to spend two days in the town jail while a judge reviewed the matter. 'I am a free man,' I concluded.

'Are you?' Trish asked slyly.

'I think so, yes. Look,' I said, holding

up my feet. 'New boots — the right size this time. I've heard that some girls don't like big feet.'

'Where did you hear that?' she asked, leaning her head against my shoulder as the last light of sunset smoldered in the darkening skies.

'Here and there,' I said, running my palm over her frizzy blond hair before letting it rest on her arm.

'What else do you hear — here and there?' she asked, turning those deep blue eyes up to me.

'Oh, that I'm kind of a funny-looking guy.'

'Yes, what else?' she prompted, her smile deepening.

'That I'm a fine-looking specimen,' I said, and she turned her lips up to be kissed, murmuring:

'That you are, Giles Clanahan, that you are.'

We do hope that you have enjoyed reading this large print book.

Did you know that all of our titles are available for purchase?

We publish a wide range of high quality large print books including:
Romances, Mysteries, Classics
General Fiction
Non Fiction and Westerns

Special interest titles available in large print are:
The Little Oxford Dictionary
Music Book, Song Book
Hymn Book, Service Book

Also available from us courtesy of Oxford University Press:
Young Readers' Dictionary
(large print edition)
Young Readers' Thesaurus
(large print edition)

For further information or a free brochure, please contact us at:
Ulverscroft Large Print Books Ltd.,
The Green, Bradgate Road, Anstey,
Leicester, LE7 7FU, England.
Tel: (00 44) **0116 236 4325**
Fax: (00 44) **0116 234 0205**

Other titles in the
Linford Western Library:

THE BUFFALO GUN

Ken Brompton

Arrow Ridge is a cattle town, its ranges owned by Clay Glandon, ruthless boss of the Big Three outfit. Homesteaders are driven off their land by his men. Only Tom Cardigan's outfit, the TT, will fight for what is theirs. Then, armed with a powerful buffalo gun, Will Keever arrives in town. His reputation as a gunslinger brings unease to those fearing retribution . . . Keever's on a mission — and that mission will bring him into deadly conflict with Glandon.

RAWHIDE RIDER

Dale Mike Rogers

Seasoned gunfighter Rawhide Jones quits working for Diamond Jim Brady to start a new life as a lawman, far from Laredo, in the border town of Santa Maria. But Brady sets his gunmen on Jones's trail to kill him: nobody quits Diamond Jim Brady and lives to tell the tale. Can Rawhide Jones turn the tables on his evil boss? With the help of Marshal Ethan Parker and his two sons, Jones tries to do the impossible and live.

DAKOTA DEATH

Billy Hall

Cotton Lang, astride his horse, knew it could be suicide to ride across the open stretch of ground. Yet his promised bride was in great peril from the twisted love of an insane suitor. Could he yet save her? Braced against the expected volley of bullets, he spurred his mount on. Now dangerously exposed and riding low and fast, nothing less than a miracle would let him survive to even learn his sweetheart's fate.

HOT LEAD, COLD HEART

Matthew P. Mayo

His Honor Newland Pontiff III, late of Exeter Territorial Prison, presides over Cayuse Falls and his vast tract of land. He has ambitious plans for the town, but a demon from his past looms on the horizon . . . Mason, mankiller and vigilante hero, has come to settle one last score with the man who'd wronged the famous 'killer of killers'. Nothing will stop him from seeing this last mission through to its end — an end he knows he won't survive.